TAKE ME HOME

A LODGE SERIES NOVEL

J.H. CROIX

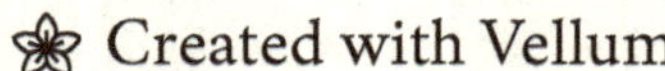 Created with Vellum

Dedication

DBC...you made me believe in my dreams.

Sign up for my newsletter for information on new releases & get a FREE copy of one of my books!

http://jhcroixauthor.com/subscribe/

Follow me!
jhcroix@jhcroix.com
https://amazon.com/author/jhcroix
https://www.bookbub.com/authors/j-h-croix
https://www.facebook.com/jhcroix

Reader note: *Take Me Home is an updated title for Christmas on the Last Frontier.*

Marley Adams walked up the old ski trail, taking in the view around her. The air held a bite of winter though fall had yet to entirely pass. Cresting the top of the trail where an abandoned ski lift sat, she turned and looked behind her. Her breath caught in her throat. Kachemak Bay lay sparkling in the sun. Mountains rose behind it on the far shore, snow-tipped and bright. She was home. Home was Diamond Creek, Alaska, a fishing village and tourist mecca in Southcentral Alaska. Breathtaking views, wildlife galore, and a tight-knit community of independent, hardy souls. The place she couldn't wait to get away from once she graduated high school. Today, she let her heart soak it in, the one and only place that ever felt like home.

She breathed in the bracing autumn air, scented with spruce and the hint of snow to come. The ground danced with color. Most of fall in Alaska happened underfoot as the landscape was heavily forested with evergreens. She turned around and eyed the ski lift. The lift swayed and creaked in the breeze. It felt like a lifetime ago when her parents had brought her up here with her sister to ski when they were little girls. The exhilaration of rushing down the bunny slope and tumbling into the soft net at the bottom was vivid in her memory. Sometime during her childhood, the ski lodge had closed and stayed empty all the years since.

Curiosity drew her to walk up to the tiny building by the lift. She wiped her arm over the smudged window and peered inside. A woodstove sat in the corner and a bench along one wall. A first aid kit was on the floor and a discarded jacket on the bench.

"Excuse me, are you aware you're trespassing?"

Marley leapt away from the window

with a squeak, whirling around to find a man leaning against the corner of the building. The man in question had short brown hair, gray eyes, sharp features, and a body that looked as if it had been sculpted in stone. Even though it was chilly enough for her to wear a lightweight jacket, he wore nothing over the t-shirt that hugged his muscled chest and arms. His legs were rock-hard and encased in sleek running pants. He looked as if he was out for a run. His gray eyes held hers. They were bright gray, as if they held lightning inside. His energy was potent masculinity. He didn't seem un-friendly, but neither did he appear welcom-ing. Against all reason, her body hummed at the sight of him. He was just…pure man.

"You startled me," she finally replied.

The man arched a brow and remained silent.

"Um, I hiked up the old ski trail. I didn't know that was a problem. We used to do it all the time when I was growing up."

The man nodded slowly. His gray eyes left her and traveled around the view, landing back on the small building he leaned against. "Right. Should have guessed that," he finally said.

Marley had never seen this man and though she'd lived away from Diamond Creek for over a decade, she came home for visits every year and knew most of the locals. If she didn't know them, her parents did. As far as she knew, no one had lived at Last Frontier Lodge for years. Residents still lamented its closure.

"Are you from around here?" she finally asked.

The man's mouth tightened. If she'd known him, she might have thought sadness flashed through his eyes.

"Depends on how you define that."

"I grew up in Diamond Creek. I used to ski here when I was a little girl. I haven't lived in town for a while, but last I knew, this place was closed and empty." She took a breath, gathering her courage. Her heart raced wildly, and she struggled to keep her composure. Whoever this man was, he had a hell of an effect on her. She couldn't even think clearly enough to introduce herself. "I'm Marley Adams. I live down the road from here," she finally said, gesturing vaguely in the direction of the little cabin on her parents' property where she'd recently moved.

Those gray eyes landed on her again. For a minute, she thought he wasn't going to respond. He cleared his throat. "I'm Gage Hamilton. My grandparents used to own this place. I was born in Diamond Creek, but my parents moved away when I was little. My, uh…" He paused and closed his eyes, grimacing slightly. When he opened his eyes again, she knew for sure what she saw was sadness. "…grandmother died recently and left the lodge to me and my younger siblings. I always loved it here when we came to visit, so I moved here. I'm planning to fix the place up and reopen, hopefully this winter."

"Oh. I'm so sorry about your grandmother," Marley said, uncertain what else to offer.

Gage nodded tightly. "Thanks. I was pretty close to her. Still getting used to the fact that she's gone."

Marley nodded, curiosity swirling inside, but she sensed now wasn't the time to ask the many questions as she had. "It's great you're planning to reopen the ski lodge. People still talk about it back when it was open. Aside from staying busy with locals, this place was hopping all winter long with tourists."

"That's what I'm hoping for." He paused and glanced at her again, his eyes softer. "I didn't mean to sound harsh when I asked about the trespassing thing. I came up for a run and didn't know who you were, so…"

"Oh, it's okay. You should know plenty of locals hike up here and use the old trails for cross-country skiing. It's not like people don't know someone else owns it, it's just no one's been here for so long, people figure it's okay."

Gage nodded slowly. "I was thinking maybe I should make some kind of announcement, but I haven't quite sorted out the details yet."

"Oh. Well, as soon as word travels that you're here and plan to reopen, you might want to be ready for lots of people showing up to say hi," she said wryly. "Diamond Creek's a small town. This is big news."

Gage smiled, and Marley thought she might swoon. Dear God, he had a dangerous smile. When he wasn't smiling, he had that whole, smoldering sexy and kind of intimidating vibe—just enough to keep her body in check. When he smiled, her body spun like a top inside—heat and electricity swirling. His eyes crinkled at the corners, the gray brightening and his mouth softening.

Get a grip, Marley. You've known this man for less than five minutes. If she let her body talk, all she could think about was what it would feel like to run her hands over his body, which was nothing short of a miracle. Though if she touched him, she'd likely melt on the spot.

Gage cleared his throat. "So, how far away do you live from here?"

"About a quarter mile down the road from the entrance to the lodge. My parents own about ten acres adjacent to the lodge. Their house is further down the road. I moved into a small cabin they used to rent out to tourists in the summer. It's tiny, but it's got everything I need."

Gage nodded. "Well, feel free to walk around here as much as you want. I suppose I'd better come up with some kind of plan to handle the locals hikers, huh?"

Marley shrugged. "People won't expect to be able to do whatever they want once you get this place up and running. So you needn't worry. You might want to notify the town hall and maybe put a notice up in the paper. Otherwise, someone being helpful might call the police if they don't know who you are and see you around the property."

Gage threw his head back with a laugh. Her stomach burst full of butterflies. She shook her head and forced herself to look away.

"I'll take it as a good sign that I have to worry about that." Gage followed her gaze out over the bay. "Well, I'm gonna keep running. Sounds like I'll see you around."

She nodded. "I'm sure you will. If you need anything, just stop by. You can see my place from the entrance to the lodge. It's the little cabin with a red roof sitting on the hill nearby."

Gage grinned. "I've seen it. Well, I'm off. Enjoy your walk," he said with a quick wave before he took off running. He went around the ski lift and turned up onto the next trail nearby—a much steeper and more advanced trail—and proceeded to run up at a steady pace. Marley had never run up that trail, but she knew without a doubt it would be grueling. He ran without his pace changing. No wonder he was in such good shape. She finally turned away and began her descent, the view stretching before her.

For the first time in months, she obsessed about something other than the crash and burn of her grand plans to make something of herself. Gage filled her mind—his rock hard body, his sensual mouth...and whoever he was behind his guarded nature.

* * *

GAGE PUSHED himself up the trail, his legs finally beginning to tire when he reached the top and paused beside another ski lift. He turned and looked behind him. He could see Marley walking down the trail below. He'd seen her long before she paused at the small building between trails. He'd only been at the ski lodge for a week, but he'd already memorized the pattern of trails and had been cutting across between two trails when he heard her walking. He'd paused in the edge of the woods and watched her. Her auburn hair glinted in the sun. Curiosity drew him to approach her. Why he felt the need to start off by confronting her about trespassing was beyond him. He shook his head. Not exactly the best way to introduce himself to his new neighbor.

From a distance, he'd thought she was beautiful. Up close, she took his breath away. Her wavy auburn hair was paired with forest green eyes, a pert nose, and a sensual mobile mouth—so kissable, he'd had to restrain himself. To make his body tread the edge of embarrassing himself, her body was flat out beautiful—curvy and athletic at once. She'd worn a green fleece jacket zipped halfway, which revealed a thin cotton shirt pulled tight across her breasts, her nipples peaked in the chilly air. From there, her waist dipped then curved into lush hips and strong legs hugged by her fitted leggings. She'd seemed entirely oblivious to the effect she had on him. Wearing his form-fitting running clothes had forced him to rein his body in and required so much attention, he knew he'd come across as a little too brusque. As he watched her walk down the trail, her auburn hair caught in the wind, flying wild behind her.

Marley. He turned the name over in his mind. It suited her though he couldn't say why since he barely knew her. He watched her until she rounded a curve in the trail and vanished from sight. With a sigh, he glanced around. The building beside this stopping point for the ski lift was also in dire need of a new coat of paint. He turned in a circle. The vantage point up here offered a three hundred and sixty degree view. Kachemak Bay lay glittering under the sun in one direction, Cook Inlet could be seen beyond that with Mount Augustine, a volcano, rising in the waters. In the other direction lay Mount Illiamna, another volcano. Southcentral Alaska lay within the Ring of Fire, an area within the Pacific basin where over seventy-five percent of the world's active and dormant volcanoes lay. As a little boy, Gage had loved this detail about his birthplace.

Returning to Alaska and his grandparent's ski lodge was a childhood dream. His parents had moved away when he and his four younger siblings were little. They went to visit Last Frontier Lodge every summer until his grandmother had closed down the lodge after his grandfather passed away. She'd moved to Bellingham, Washington to live with his parents until she passed away. Gage had long ago let go of his childhood dream to return to Alaska because life...

happened. Dreams turned into fragments of hope and hope was hard to find for him anymore. He'd recently retired from the Navy after years of active duty as a Navy SEAL and had been struggling to find a way for life to make sense.

Gage had been surprised to learn his grandmother had left the lodge to him and his siblings since he hadn't even known it was still in the family. He'd inherited the largest share of the lodge with her will stipulating the lodge must be reopened within one year, or they would be required to sell it and divide the profits. He'd assumed she'd sold it as she rarely spoke of it. At loose ends and searching for something to give his life meaning again, he hadn't hesitated for a minute to move to Alaska. The neglected state of the ski lodge would give him something to focus on beyond what he'd stared down on one of his last missions.

He took a last look around and began jogging slowly down the trail. An eagle flew across the trail ahead of him, its wings casting a wide shadow on the ground. Magpies chattered in the trees. When he reached the lodge again, he jogged down the drive to the road and looked toward the cabin he now knew to be Marley's. It was hard to miss with its bright red roof practically glowing amongst the deep green spruce trees surrounding it. He turned and looked at the sign for the lodge. It hung at a drunken angle, one of the chains holding it up broken. The lettering on the sign was faded—something else to replace. He looked at Marley's cabin again, sitting on a small rise, a cheery picturesque home. Her auburn hair, green eyes, and sensual mouth flashed in his mind. The mere flicker of her and his body reacted.

CHAPTER 2

*M*arley stopped her car at the end of her drive and glanced up at Last Frontier Lodge. From the road, it wasn't obvious anyone lived there. Knowing Gage was there set her pulse thrumming. *Seriously, Marley? You're acting like an idiot with a crush. You barely know the guy. Not to mention, there's no way a guy like him would be interested in you. Way out of your league.* She shook her head sharply and turned onto the winding road that led down the hill to town. She'd only been here about a week and had yet to mentally adjust. Her parents meant well, but they were driving her mad with their daily calls to check in and job suggestions.

Her move back home had been unplanned and abrupt. She'd graduated from high school and headed to college in Seattle, filled with dreams of making it big in the technology world. She'd never wanted the money, but she'd desperately wanted to feel like a success. All through school, she'd been a computer geek of the highest order, long before it became fashionable. She'd headed to Seattle with stars in her eyes. Sometimes cliché's fit, and in this case, her starry dream was she'd get her business degree and make a splash in the tech world. In the big scheme of things, she'd done okay. But she'd tried to break into the world of technology as a woman from a tiny town in Alaska. She'd become well-versed in the rampant sexism in the tech field. She'd made it farther than many women and made a good salary as a code developer for an app company in Seattle.

Right when she thought she might have enough money put away to break out on her own, she'd walked into her apartment in the midst of a robbery. Her surprise appearance had only made the situation worse with the masked robber whacking her across the face with his gun and shoving her in a corner before he commenced to finish what he started. She'd fallen apart afterwards though she'd tried her damnedest not to. Sleepless nights, constant anxiety, and the loss of concentration made her job all but impossible. At thirty, she found herself without a job and afraid to live in her apartment.

Lost and confused, she returned to Diamond Creek, the only place that felt like home—that felt safe. Her hopes and dreams were tattered, but she was sleeping a few hours every night now. Anger sometimes choked her. She hated feeling so fragile and having her dreams ripped away from her. She'd spent most of her life being proud of how independent she was, unafraid to see what the world had to offer. Now, she just wanted to hunker down and hide. Though a part of her was happy to be home, she wished she'd come home on her own terms. She took a shaky breath and forced her mind away from her problems.

Marley looked around as she drove into town. Diamond Creek had grown since she'd moved away. Though she'd visited every year, she hadn't taken time to explore town much. There were now three grocery stores in town, and the multitude of art galleries, restaurants and shops catering to tourists had ballooned. She was meeting her sister, Lacey, for coffee at Misty Mountain Café. Lacey was two years younger than her and had happily returned to Diamond Creek after she finished college in Juneau.

Marley walked into Misty Mountain, smiling at how little had changed. The café was in a renovated Quonset hut, one of many scattered around Alaska, relics from World War II when the huts had been used for military installations throughout Alaska due to its proximity to the Pacific Rim. The owners had transformed the utilitarian steel tube-shaped building with finished walls and decorative timber beams. Cheerful paint colors and curtains brightened the space with local artwork lining the walls. She looked around and found Lacey in the corner. She waved and headed to order her coffee.

Threading her way through the scattered tables, she grinned when she reached Lacey and slid into the chair across from her.

"Hey there," she said with a lift of her cup in greeting.

"Hey yourself," Lacey replied. "How's it going over at the little red inn?"

That was Lacey's affectionate name for the cabin Marley had commandeered on her parents' property. The cabin wasn't red, but the roof was, so the name stuck. Marley shrugged. "Pretty good. I forgot how amazing the view is from there."

Lacey nodded, her chestnut ponytail bouncing along. "The rise from the hill makes it feel like you can reach over and touch the glacier across the bay."

Lacey paused and waved to someone who entered the café. Yet another person Marley didn't recognize.

"So how are you? Any more trips planned before the snow flies?" Marley asked.

Lacey was an outdoor guide. She spent most of summer away from Diamond Creek with brief stays in between treks to the backcountry. She wasn't a hunting or fishing guide, but an expert backcountry guide for elite hikers who wanted to experience hiking without easy access. Lacey didn't consider anything hiking unless she had to fly in. She was tough as nails. Marley had the brains, and Lacey the brawn. Lacey was pure athlete and dressed the part. Her body was toned and fit, and she could have easily been a model for outdoor clothing companies. Except for the fact that her clothing was usually worn to shreds within weeks of getting it.

Lacey nodded, her green eyes, so similar to Marley's, taking on a gleam. "One more. Heading up to the refuge for a week. My friend Cal is running this trip with me. The early snow is already flying that far north."

"You mean the Arctic National Wildlife Refuge?"

At Lacey's nod, Marley continued. "Wow. That's way up there. Have you been there this late in the year before?"

Lacey shook her head. "Nope. It's safer than going in the thick of summer. The grizzlies are already hibernating."

Marley shook her head. As if grizzly bears were all Lacey would need to worry about. Marley wouldn't mind finding a way to siphon some of Lacey's courage. She'd never thought of herself as a frightened person, but getting robbed at gunpoint made her afraid of too many shadows.

Lacey nibbled on a muffin and pushed a plate across the table to Marley.

"For me?" Marley asked.

"Of course! It's your favorite—spinach and ham pinwheel."

Marley almost burst into tears. It was ridiculous how emotionally edgy she was these days. The mundane moment made her feel safe, something she'd never take for granted again. She took a slow breath and tried to gather herself.

"You okay?" Lacey's voice was soft.

Marley nodded, the press of tears subsiding. "Yeah. It's just...good to be home."

Lacey looked at her carefully. "So, what now?"

"What do you mean?"

"I mean, you're here now. What are you going to do next? Mom and Dad are going to be super helpful, so either you come up with your own plan, or else," Lacey said with a wry grin.

Marley sighed. "Working on it. My plan right now is to try to do what I meant to do in Seattle—start my own app company. I have plenty of connections. All I need is an internet connection to do what I need. I have some money saved up, so I figure I might as well try."

Lacey grinned. "Awesome! That's what I was hoping you'd do."

"Really?" Marley felt so disoriented since the robbery that she questioned everything she did. Between that and years of witnessing how hard it was to break into the market with anything new, she'd lost the confidence she'd once had in herself.

Lacey took a sip of coffee. "Of course! I always wondered why you thought you had to make a go of it in the city. You can do everything you need to right here, and avoid the bullshit of all the hobnobs telling you what you can and can't do."

Marley nodded slowly. "Right. Maybe I should have asked your advice about ten years ago," she said ruefully.

"Nah. You had to figure it out yourself."

Marley pondered Lacey's point. Marley had been determined to show her stuff somewhere outside of Diamond Creek. She wished upon wish it hadn't taken a robbery to shake the foundation of her life, but coming home felt so good.

"Hey, did you know that Last Frontier Lodge was reopening?" Marley asked, ready to move on from discussing her life.

Lacey's eyes widened. "No way! Where did you hear that?"

Marley filled her in on her encounter

with Gage, minus the details about how drool-worthy handsome and sexy he was.

Lacey leaned back in her chair. "That's big news! I'm stoked. We'll finally have somewhere to ski again nearby. Last time that place was open, we were so little, all we could do was coast down the bunny slopes. Now we can do some real skiing. What's he like? The guy who inherited the place?"

Marley paused and pictured Gage—his body, all hard muscle, his eyes like lightning, his mouth sensual and full, and his reserved manner. She flushed at the mere thought of him.

"Oh my, Marley, you have a thing," Lacey said with a sly grin.

"I do not!" she replied, trying and failing miserably at making her blush go away. She was so rusty at relationships, the idea of having a 'thing' for anyone intimidated the hell out of her.

Lacey giggled. "All I did was ask you what he's like, and you got all quiet and dreamy. Don't you hate how easy you blush?"

Marley rolled her eyes, her face and neck hot. "You do too!"

"That's how come I know you probably

hate it," Lacey retorted. "Okay, so you've got the serious hots for him. As far as I'm concerned, you are in need of a distraction, and this Gage guy might be exactly what you need."

"Um, pretty sure he's out of my league."

Lacey waved a hand dismissively. "You're totally hot, but you had your nose buried so deep in books and computers that you've never noticed. When's the last time you went on a date?"

Marley tried to recall. After a long moment, she gave up. "I don't know. You know how it was for me. I worked all the time. Sixty, seventy-hour weeks were the norm. There wasn't much time for dating."

Lacey's grin faded as she looked across the table. Her green eyes softened and she absently twirled her ponytail around a finger. "I hate what happened to you and it pisses me off that you're feeling bad about freaking out about it, but I'm really glad you're home. I didn't want it to happen this way, but I'll take it." She paused, considering her words. "I'm not the mushy sort, you know that. But if you need to talk, I'm here. And if there's only one thing I can tell you, it's that you have to know anyone would be scared if they went through what you did. Stop beating yourself up about it."

Marley looked over at her sister and wondered how Lacey understood her so well. They were so different. Marley took a deep breath and closed her eyes. Opening them, she met Lacey's. "I'm working on it, okay?"

Lacey nodded. After a moment, her grin returned. "Maybe you should offer to help Gage out with the lodge? Be a friendly neighbor and all that."

Marley started to shake her head.

Lacey held her hand up. "Or you could skip the preliminaries and screw his brains out."

Marley choked on her coffee.

CHAPTER 3

Gage walked down the driveway. He was tired, dusty and sweaty from an entire morning dedicated to cleaning and repairing inside the lodge. Given how many years the lodge sat empty, the inside areas were in surprisingly decent shape though covered in dust. His grandmother had left the place with all the windows boarded up and the doors secured. Throughout the lodge's many rooms, he'd only encountered a few mice infestations. The inside was in dire need of updated furnishings, along with some minor repairs, but the essentials were sound. The outside was where he had more work to do. He'd ordered the exterior paint yesterday from the local hardware store.

After a long morning inside, he needed some fresh air. He reached the head of the drive and eyed the sign at the entrance, a large wooden sign mounted between two posts. The chain was broken on one side. He tugged the new chain he'd brought with him out of his tool belt and wiped his face on his sleeve. He quickly got to work replacing the chain, stepping back once it was done.

"Well, your sign doesn't look drunk anymore," a feminine voice called out.

Gage turned to find Marley walking up the road toward him. Her auburn hair fell around her shoulders in loose waves. She wore running shoes, fleece leggings and a t-shirt that pulled tightly across her breasts. When she reached him, she put her hands on her hips and tilted her head, eying the sign. All she did was stand there and his body kicked into gear. His breath hitched as he imagined what it would feel like to run his hands along her curves.

"I'd say it's level," she said with a grin.

"Would you tell me if it wasn't?" he countered. He wanted to keep her talking—about anything. Because that meant she'd keep standing here beside him. *Get a grip, dude. You're about to lose it over a woman you barely know.*

She pursed her lips, those full, sensuous lips a magnet for his eyes. He had to force himself to look up. Of course, that meant looking into her bright green eyes.

"I would. I mean, you're trying to fix it, right? You seem like someone who'd want to do it right."

Gage couldn't help but grin. "I definitely want to do it right. No sense in half-measures." He paused and looked to the bay. The sun was high in the early afternoon sky. Clouds drifted lazily in front of the mountains. A cool breeze gusted when he looked back at Marley, blowing her hair wild. She ignored the tousled waves. Her nearness kick-started his pulse. Without the slightest effort, she made his body stand up and take notice.

"What brings you up here?" he asked.

"When I came home a few minutes ago, I saw you working on the sign. Just thought I'd see how it's going."

Her genuine curiosity and friendliness threw him. He couldn't say why, but it wasn't something he experienced much beyond his family. After several years in the military, his mother had tried to point out that he'd become less approachable. He'd ignored her though part of him knew she was right. Marley didn't seem to notice and carried on as if checking on a neighbor she barely knew was perfectly normal. In a place such as Diamond Creek, it probably was. But this world wasn't the world he'd lived in for years.

He damn sure didn't know how to manage his attraction to her. After too many years of high-level missions as a Navy SEAL, women weren't something he considered. His life was all work and no play. His last girlfriend had tactfully ended their relationship. He'd been too quiet, too withdrawn and definitely not emotionally available. Yet, he hadn't encountered a single woman who affected him the way Marley did. And Marley—she did it without the slightest effort, no artifice, and appeared oblivious to the effect she had on him.

Looking over at her, he watched her absently twirl an auburn curl around her finger. When she caught him looking at her, she flushed and dropped her hand. He realized he'd yet to reply to her.

"If you're wondering how it's going, it's been busy. I've gotten the lay of the land, so to speak, and now I have to get to work. I was hoping I'd be able to get the lodge up and running by the holidays, but I'm not so sure. I'm focusing on the outside work from today on, so I can get new exterior paint on before it's too cold. After that, I have to decide what to do inside."

Marley tilted her head. "I can see the buildings need a new coat of paint, but what do you have to do inside?"

"Gram did a good job of boarding the place up, but it's dusty and needs a hell of a cleaning. I have to decide what to do about the furnishings too. This place was modern roughly twenty years ago, but now it's like walking into a time warp. I'm not thinking that's a great way to start if I want to make a go of it with the lodge. Assuming I can take care of everything in time for the holidays, then I have to figure out the website situation. This place closed long before the internet existed. My sisters insist I'd better plan to get something up online sooner rather than later, but I'm lost in that area. I don't want to start too soon, or before I know the lodge will be ready to take reservations." He ran a hand through his hair and sighed. The repairs, even trying to handle the decorating inside, he figured he could somehow make it work. The online thing—forget it. He'd argued with his sisters about it, but they were adamant he'd be silly to think he could get a ski lodge up and running without some kind of online presence.

"I could help with that," Marley said.

Gage looked at her, her beauty hijacking his brain for a second before he forced himself to focus. "Huh?"

The effect she had on him was flat ridiculous. He was a man of precision and focus. He'd handled high-stress, high-pressure missions for years. Yet, all he could say to Marley was 'huh.'

She nodded, a strand of hair blowing across her face. Since she didn't offer further clarification, appearing to think he understood her, he had to ask another question.

"What do you mean you can help with that?"

"I mean, I can help you build your website. If you tell me what you want, we can have one up and running pretty quick."

Gage stared at her. "You can do that?"

Marley smiled and flushed. "I'm a programmer. Building a website isn't that hard. I don't mean to take sides, but your sisters are right. You need a website, and you need it up and running before you're ready to open. If you don't do that, you won't have a way to take reservations and set up a payment system. No one will even know the Last Frontier Lodge exists unless they happen to live in Diamond Creek. The locals love this place, but they aren't your bread and butter. You need a presence online as soon as you can get it. You can't leave it until the last minute. We can set it up so you post updates about when it will be ready to open."

Gage stared at her for so long, he didn't notice until she started to shift on her feet and glance away.

She cleared her throat. "Sorry if I overstepped there. It's just..."

"You didn't overstep. Sorry if it seemed like I thought you did. The whole website thing is so out of my territory that I kind of hoped I could ignore it. But if you're really offering to help..." He battled the smile building inside. Marley's offer was two-fold for him. He needed the help she was offering, but more than that he couldn't help the anticipation of having an excuse to be around her.

Marley's smile made his heart clench and his pulse gallop away again.

"I'm really offering. Tell me when you have some time. I can stop by with my laptop and we can get started."

"We?"

Marley threw her head back with a laugh. "Not to worry. 'We' doesn't mean you have to do anything other than take a look at some other sites with me and tell me what you like."

"I think I can handle that. How about this afternoon?" He startled himself with the offer. An unfamiliar part of him was making itself known—a part that didn't fit the tidy, controlled compartments he'd lived within during his years as a Navy SEAL. Impulsive, last-minute decisions weren't part of the planned life he'd lived for years. But he didn't care to question himself. Beyond legitimately needing her help with something he'd planned to ignore, he couldn't deny how much he simply wanted to be around her.

Marley held his eyes for a long moment

before nodding slowly. "This afternoon is fine. What time?"

Gage calculated what he had left to do and the fact that he desperately needed a shower. "Four?"

"Four works for me. I'll head back to my place and see you then." She gave a small wave and turned to look at the sign once more. "It's nice to see that," she said softly.

"What do you mean?"

"I missed skiing at the lodge. If you get to know people around town, you'll find plenty of people are going to be beside themselves about this place opening again."

At that, she turned again and started down the slope to her cabin. "See you soon," she called, her voice lifting above the breeze.

He watched her go, her arms swinging at her sides, her hair a blowing curtain behind her.

* * *

MARLEY STOOD by the table where her laptop sat and stared blankly at it. A vision of Gage filled her mind. He'd been wearing faded blue jeans, his leather tool belt hanging loosely at his hips, with another t-shirt that molded over his body like a glove. Sweaty and dusty, he'd been a sight to behold. Somehow, she'd remembered her manners and managed to engage in normal conversation with him. Then she'd gone and offered to help him with the website for the ski lodge. She hadn't even been thinking. It wasn't that she didn't want to help. It would be minimal effort on her part. Problem was Gage drove her to distraction and made her want things she couldn't have. He was probably accustomed to beautiful women, not brainy girls with an outdoorsy streak. But now she'd gone and said she'd be there this afternoon. And a tiny part of her was thrilled!

What the hell were you thinking? Too close for comfort. You're going to end up half-drooling over him and look like an idiot.

Lacey's teasing that Gage might be the distraction she needed came to mind. But Marley couldn't go there. Distraction or not, she was not his type. No way. He was all manly, sexy, and smoldering. She was the girl who buried her nose in books and computers. Though she didn't know his story yet, he exuded dark and mysterious, precise and in control. If he knew she checked her locks repeatedly every evening and jumped at the sound of unknown noises, he'd think she was a bumbling idiot.

But you can whip up a website for him in no time. That's all this has to be. You'll be a friendly, good neighbor and keep your distance after that.

A few hours later, Marley walked to her car, set her computer bag on the passenger seat and drove up to the lodge. The afternoon light was fading rapidly. With summer gone, the fall nights were coming earlier and earlier. She hadn't been home in the fall since she'd moved away over a decade ago. She'd forgotten how much she loved it—the cool bite in the air, the sharp scent of spruce, the sense that the quiet of winter was just ahead.

Moments later, she knocked on the main entrance door to the ski lodge. Gage opened the door almost immediately. He gestured her inside. Marley looked around as she walked through the entryway. The inside was as Gage indicated: a time warp. The furniture was covered with plastic, so she couldn't see what was underneath, but the overall feel of the space was as she remembered, including a faded calendar on the wall behind the desk with pictures of mountains. The calendar was open to the month of October, the year nineteen ninety-four. Faded harvest decorations remained on the reception desk. She followed Gage down a hallway, passed through the restaurant area and into an office in the back. This room had been thoroughly cleaned and was furnished sparingly with a basic black desk and new leather office chair. A round table was situated nearby with chairs surrounding it.

She set her laptop on the table and looked around for an outlet. She met Gage's eyes. "Do you have internet, or should I run back home to get my portable wireless device?"

He surprised her by nodding. "Oh yeah. I may be clueless when it comes to building websites, but I like my cable and stay in touch with friends and family online. Got to be a habit when I was in the military."

So he was military. It didn't surprise her at all, given his near physical perfection and the sense of precision he exuded. She filed that detail away and quickly logged onto his network. Gage drew a chair up beside her and watched as she pulled up various ski lodge websites. At first, he was quiet, but he quickly became focused, pointing out websites he did and didn't like.

Not much later, Marley was contemplating how to find a graceful way to get out of there. Gage appeared oblivious to the effect he had on her. He had tugged his chair close to hers and frequently leaned over her shoulder to look at the screen as she built a template for the site. His nearness was distracting beyond belief. She was hot and flushed. The few times she turned to look at him, her pulse surged. His gray eyes were like the sky before a storm. His cheekbones looked sculpted from stone, his jaw was strong and square, and his lips...well, she couldn't remember ever noticing a man's lips. But when she looked at his, all she could think about was how they might feel on hers. His smile was rare, but when it happened, it tightened her nipples and spun a burst of wet heat—a ping of sensation that spiraled into the heat of desire she couldn't seem to control around him.

She managed to keep herself half focused on what they were doing, but just barely. *Thank god you could do this with your eyes closed. Otherwise, you'd be useless about now.*

You need to move away from him. Oh my god, his arm feels sooo good. Get a grip!

Gage leaned over to point at something on the screen.

"Can you make it have a button like that one?" he asked, gesturing to another site she had up beside the one she was working on.

The heat and hardness of his arm practically singed her skin. She'd taken her jacket off—like a fool—and he kept brushing against the skin on her bare arm. She looked to where he was pointing.

"Oh yeah, got it." She quickly pulled up options for an icon and selected a bright green button for reservations. "How's that?"

"Oh, wow. That's it. It works?"

Marley made the mistake of turning to look at him. He turned exactly when she did, their eyes colliding. The gray of his eyes flickered and darkened. She felt the heat of a blush race up her neck and face. Her pulse pounded, butterflies thronged in her center, and she couldn't seem to get enough air.

The space between them felt electrified. She was so rattled, she started to push back from the table. When she went to move, Gage put his hand on her arm. The warm heat of his palm curling around her forearm was so delicious, she gasped. She couldn't break away from the smoky intensity of his gaze. She tried to remember his question, but she couldn't. When she opened her mouth to try to say something, he moved swiftly. His lips came against hers in a fierce rush. Her body craved his touch so desperately, she didn't stop to think. Her mouth opened under his instantly. The moment she opened to him, his touch shifted from fast and furious to slow and devastating. The intense rush spiraled into a drugging passion.

Gage kissed with a thoroughness Marley had never experienced. He explored her mouth completely, his tongue sweeping inside. He pulled away just enough to catch her bottom lip between his teeth before taking her mouth again in a deep, open-mouthed kiss. Long pulse-pounding, breath-stealing moments later, he pulled away. Dazed and aroused beyond measure, Marley opened her eyes to find his inches away. She couldn't look away. He looked startled. His pulse was visible in his neck, which relieved her only in that he seemed as out of control as she felt.

He leaned back slightly. His hand remained on her arm, his touch sending waves of heat through her. He cleared his throat.

Certain he must have lost his mind by kissing her, Marley decided she'd best get out ahead of this. "I…" She had to stop and clear her throat, her voice raspy. "I'm, um, not sure what happened. I'm sure you didn't mean…"

Gage put his finger on her lips, the touch burning into her, pinwheels of desire spinning inside. His smoky gaze was so intently focused on her, she had to fight the urge to squirm.

"I meant to do exactly what I did," he said bluntly. His finger fell from her lips.

Stunned at his words and scrambling to gather her thoughts, she watched his hand come to rest on his muscled thigh. Even his hands turned her on—strong with evidence of hard work. A faded scar arced across the back of his hand as it flexed around his thigh. She brought her eyes back to his. "Oh, well then…I don't know…"

His lips quirked in a small smile and her heart soared.

"You don't know what?"

"I don't know what that was about."

"Maybe I don't either, but I know this—

I've wanted to kiss you every time I saw you, so I finally decided to stop fighting it," he said simply.

"Oh."

Marley tried to wrap her brain around the fact that this man, who was practically calendar material and all kinds of sexy, had wanted to kiss her since the moment he saw her. She supposed it was good they had that in common. She looked into his eyes again and saw a warm glint. A giggle bubbled up and next thing she knew she was laughing so hard she couldn't stop.

Gage watched Marley's green eyes go wide and then she started to laugh. Her laugh was throaty. He hadn't meant to kiss her in the sense that he planned it. But when he met her eyes—those gorgeous green eyes that made him think of a forest dappled with sun—he wanted to kiss her so badly it was all he wanted. In that split second, he abandoned his reservations and decided it was worth it to see if she felt as good as she looked. He'd spent the hour or so she'd been here dancing on the edge of a raging hard on. He was relieved as hell he was sitting down, so the blatant evidence of his arousal wasn't immediately obvious.

Now he knew. It was more than worth it and kissing her was like walking into a fire that curled and swirled around him and held him in its seductive flame. Watching her laugh made him want to kiss her again. There were only two problems: she seemed remarkably startled to hear how much he wanted her, and he had no intention of getting serious with anyone. Marley wasn't the kind of girl a man just had fun with. He didn't even do that lately either. Then, there was the double-edged sword of her being his neighbor in this small town in Alaska. He couldn't avoid her, but at the moment, he didn't think he had a chance in hell of keeping his hands off of her.

Her throaty laugh slowed and her eyes met his, dancing with warmth.

"Care to share what's so funny?" he asked.

Her lush, sensual lips quirked with a smile again. Then she sobered, her eyes flickering with uncertainty. "It surprised me so much that you said you've wanted to kiss me since you first saw me. It seemed ridiculous. I don't mean that you meant it that way, more that I couldn't believe it."

"You couldn't believe it? Have you looked in the mirror lately?"

Her eyes widened. "Um, yeah." Her cheeks flushed as she met his gaze. He sensed she wanted to look away, but she didn't. He wanted to know who planted the seeds of doubt he saw there.

"Well, I don't know what you see, but you're damn beautiful. You must not pay attention to the men I'm sure are thinking the same thing I've been thinking."

Her eyes widened further. She brushed a loose lock of hair out of her eyes. "I think I'm supposed to say thank you."

Gage had tons of questions, but decided to leave them for now.

"I also thought it was funny that we had something in common," Marley added.

"What's that?"

"I've wanted to kiss you ever since I met you." Her cheeks flushed bright red. She twirled her hair around her finger.

Her words made his heart feel strange, not to mention that his cock, barely under control, hardened at her frank statement. He closed his eyes, fighting to get his body in check. Because what he wanted was much more than a kiss, but he wasn't about to go there right now. With a kiss, he could find a way to regroup and pull back if needed. Much more and he could ruin any chance at a friendship with her.

You want a hell of a lot more than friendship. What's stopping you? Oh maybe the fact that Marley's all kinds of amazing and way too good for you. Coward.

Gage ignored the taunt inside his mind and focused on Marley and her last words. "Good to know," he replied, so damn pleased she'd wanted to kiss him too that he ignored all of his own rules—no complications, no commitments. It was easier that way. He'd already broken them with the kiss. He itched to touch her again. Her t-shirt was faded navy and pulled taut across her generous breasts. He'd give just about anything to see them. Her blush faded, but lingered in her bright cheeks. Up close, he could see tiny freckles scattered on her skin.

He forced himself to push his chair back a little and glanced at the computer screen. His eyes landed on the icon she'd added for people to click to make reservations. "So does that really work?"

Marley followed his eyes. "It will. We need to set up the back end, so when people click on this, it takes them to your payment system." Her voice started breathy and steadied as she spoke.

"I can't just have them pay when they get here?"

Marley grinned. "You could, but you might lose money that way. People are more likely to keep their reservations if they have to put down a deposit. We don't have to make it complicated. I can help you set something up for that."

Gage sighed and looked back at her. What he wanted to do was lose himself in another kiss and then some, but he knew that wasn't the wisest plan. Not now. His chest tightened at the depth of his want for Marley. He shook his head sharply. He needed to focus on something other than kissing her. The brief time he'd spent with her had made him realize why his sisters insisted he'd better get the online situation set up sooner rather than later. He had the wherewithal to do all the repair work and construction for the lodge, but the stuff Marley did with a few clicks was foreign to him. If he wanted to make the lodge come back to life, he had to be ready to do whatever it took.

She tilted her head and smiled softly. "It's not so bad. I offered to help, and I will. It's pretty easy stuff for me. You don't need to get all worried about it."

He nodded, his chest easing. "Right. We didn't talk about it, but I can pay you…"

She shook her head and started to say something, but he interjected again. "I can't do this part. At all. If it's not you, I'll have to pay someone else. I trust you, and you're already halfway there, so tell me whatever you'd normally charge someone for something like this."

She smiled slowly and started to giggle again.

"What's funny now?"

She swallowed her laugh. "I'm a programmer and I can do stuff like this, but it's not something I've ever thought about charging for. I don't even know what to say."

"I'll call someone and find out what they'd charge me and pay you that."

Marley started to say no, and Gage couldn't help it, he kissed her again. Her lips were soft, luscious and warm. And though she seemed surprised to realize he was attracted to her, she didn't let it interfere once their lips met. Her mouth opened, her tongue tangled with his. He dove straight into the cauldron. By the time he came up for air, his breath was ragged, and lust streaked through him so hard, he could barely think. When her green eyes met his, dazed with passion, it was all he could do to stop.

* * *

MARLEY WALKED up the steps to her parents' house. She knocked quickly on the kitchen door and walked inside. Her mother, Holly, was sitting at the kitchen table by the window, a laptop open in front of her. Holly looked up and smiled as soon as she saw Marley.

"Hey hon! How are you?" Holly stood and walked to the kitchen counter. "Coffee?" she asked, gesturing to the coffee pot.

"Sure," Marley replied, tugging her jacket off and tossing it over the back of a chair before she sat down. The casual occurrence of sitting down for coffee with her mother was so comforting, it elicited a wave of emotion. She wondered when her emotions would stop being so raw. It chafed at her to feel out of control and struck at the core of anger she'd felt ever since the robbery.

Holly filled a mug with coffee and joined Marley at the table. Holly had passed on her auburn hair, green eyes, and lightly freckled complexion to Marley. Her hair was piled in a loose knot atop her head. She smiled warmly as she slid the mug across the table to Marley.

Marley cupped the warm mug in her palms, chilled from the cool walk down from her cabin.

"So?" her mother asked.

"So, what?"

Holly rolled her eyes. "How are you settling in? Any word on what you're going to do for work?"

Marley sighed inside. Her mother meant well, but she wanted Marley settled and working full-time as soon as possible. Marley knew her parents were ecstatic she was back in Diamond Creek. They'd been so worried about her after what happened. But she was weary from trying to explain that the usual nine-to-five type job they were hoping she'd find wasn't exactly what she had in mind. She was determined not to let the robbery steal everything from her. She wasn't giving up her dreams, only relocating them.

She looked up and met her mother's warm green gaze. A sense of safety stole over her, something she'd never thought she'd miss until it had been ripped away from her in a flash. Sitting here in her parents' kitchen with her well-meaning and loving mother represented a simple degree of safety and warmth. She took a deep breath.

"I'm settling in okay. I don't have a ton of stuff, so the cabin's all set now. I promise, I'll just be there over the winter. By next summer, I'm sure I'll find another place."

Holly shook her head. "Honey, we told you not to worry about that. We haven't rented that cabin out in years. Consider it yours."

Marley didn't have the heart to explain that treating the cabin as hers made her feel like a failure, like she couldn't make it on her own. She needed the safety and respite of not worrying about finding a new place to live at the moment, but she had no intention of making her stay at the cabin anything other than temporary.

"I know, Mom. I'll play it by ear. How's that?"

Holly nodded as she sipped her coffee. "What's happening on the work front?"

"Well, I'm helping design the website for the Last Frontier Lodge."

Holly's eyes widened. "What? The Lodge is opening again? I haven't heard anything about it."

Marley couldn't help but feel a thrill at being in possession of gossip her mother didn't know. "Yeah. I was up there the other day walking on one of the old ski trails when I met the new owner. Well, he's not totally new. His grandparents owned the lodge, and he inherited it. It's Gage Hamilton."

Holly looked thoughtful. "Wow, he was just a boy when I last saw him. His parents used to live here, and then they moved away. That's wonderful news! When does he plan to open and how did you end up doing the website?"

Marley offered a quick summary minus the details of how deliciously sexy Gage was and definitely omitting the fact that he'd kissed her senseless. She could hardly believe it herself and had spent half the night reliving his kisses in her mind. The news got her mother off the topic of problem-solving Marley's work situation and onto reminiscing about the ski lodge.

"Have you been inside?" Holly asked a few minutes later.

Marley nodded. "Yeah. When I got started on the website, I met him there. Gage said it was like walking into a time warp, and it is. The furniture's covered up, but it looks just the same. He says he wants to open by Christmas, but he wants to redo the inside, so he's got his work cut out for him. He seems up for it though."

Holly nodded, a slow smile spreading over her face. "I can't wait to tell your dad. He used to love skiing there every weekend. If Gage gets it open in time, I know where we'll be on Christmas."

Her mother's phone buzzed. Holly glanced at the screen on her phone. "Oh hon, I have to get going. I'm covering an extra shift at the hospital."

Holly stood up and walked to the kitchen sink, gulping the rest of her coffee.

"Speaking of work, when are you planning to slow down a little?" Marley asked.

Her mother was a nurse at the hospital

and had yet to even pause in the pace of her work. Holly glanced her way and shrugged. "As long as I enjoy it, I'll keep working."

Marley started to get up, but Holly waved for her to stay put. "Finish your coffee. You don't have to leave just because I am. Our house is yours."

Though part of her resisted the comfort offered, another part of her basked in relief. Holly pecked her on the cheek and raced out the door. Marley sat at the kitchen table and looked out toward the bay and mountains. Her childhood home felt as it always did—quiet when no one was present, but humming with subtle energy. Her mother was a whirlwind, and her father constantly had projects around the house. He was a fisherman and carpenter. Marley savored the quiet and the peaceful view. Though Seattle had Mount Rainier and the Cascades nearby, she never felt the sense of wildness like she did here in Alaska. Perhaps because even where there were towns in Alaska, the wilderness dwarfed them, rather than the other way around. Snow continued to fall every night on the mountains across the bay, the peaks stark white against the blue sky now.

After she finished her coffee, she walked home through the spruce forest. When she saw the bright red roof of her cabin through the trees, she smiled. She'd always loved the cabin when she was a little girl. She and Lacey often had sleepovers there when they were old enough with her mother checking on them late at night and first thing in the morning. Though she'd come home under circumstances she wouldn't have chosen, the sense of relief she'd felt when her parents offered for her to stay at the cabin was immense. She needed to regroup and needed a place where she felt safe. Diamond Creek and the charming little cabin offered her those things.

As she crested the small rise where the cabin sat, she saw Gage's truck in the driveway. Her heart leapt and flutters swirled in her belly. He looked as if he'd been knocking on the door. He turned away and began to walk down the steps when he saw her. He waved and leaned against the railing. Marley couldn't help but appreciate the view. He wore faded jeans that hugged his muscled legs. He seemed partial to t-shirts that molded to his chest like a second skin. When she reached the bottom of the stairs and looked up, her breath caught and her pulse ricocheted. His chocolate brown hair was damp, his gray eyes smoky and focused completely on her. His mouth kicked up at the corner as she stood there.

"Hey there," he said, his voice gravelly and warm at once.

"Hey. What brings you here?" Marley managed to get a halfway polite reply out, but she had to force her brain to function enough to form words.

Gage's smile expanded, and heat unfurled through Marley's body.

"I saw your car in the drive on the way to town, and thought I'd stop by and see if you might be willing to go with me to the furniture place up in Kenai." He arched a brow when she didn't reply and continued. "I need help with figuring out what to do inside. I could use a feminine perspective. If it's left up to me, my sister says it will be black and white and boring," he said wryly, a subtle flush staining his cheeks.

Marley couldn't help but laugh. She didn't even stop to think and found herself nodding. "Sure. I can't promise you amazing results, but I'm happy to help. When are you going?"

"I was about to leave now, but I'll wait if that works better for you."

"I thought you were starting with the exterior paint. The weather's perfect for that today." Marley's body was thrilled with the idea of spending the afternoon with Gage, but her mind was leery. He got her so hot and bothered, it confused her.

"It is, but my paint won't be in until tomorrow, so I'm adjusting my plans."

Marley thought for a moment. She had no reason to say "no" seeing as she had no plans for the day other than calculating how far her savings would take her while she tried to see if she could start making money off of some of the apps she had in development. If her body had any say in the matter, she'd run to Gage's truck and spend the day in proximity to him. Her mind, on the other hand, wasn't so sure. But then she glanced up at him again, her eyes colliding with his smoky gaze, and she couldn't consider anything other than spending the day with him looking at furniture. Though it went without saying that decorating a ski lodge was definitely not her area of expertise.

CHAPTER 5

Gage followed Marley as they walked out to the parking lot. He'd quickly discovered that while she wasn't an expert at decorating, she was quite good at wrangling salespeople to do her bidding. By the end of several hours, he'd selected the set of furnishings for the entryway and other public areas. He also had some simple solutions for updating the bedroom suites and the restaurant. He made arrangements for the furniture to be delivered the following week. Marley walked ahead of him, her hips swaying and the fall of her auburn hair blowing in the wind. He imagined what it would feel like to run his hands down the curves of her hips and cup her lush bottom. His body had a good idea of how that might feel, leading him to swear to himself and stare at his boots the rest of the way to his truck. If there was one thing he wasn't accustomed to, it was not being in control. He'd underestimated his attraction to Marley. Spending a few hours with her left him scrambling to get his mind and body under control.

Marley turned to him once they were in the truck. "What now?"

"I say we drive back to Diamond Creek and celebrate with dinner." As soon as the words came out of his mouth, Gage wondered if he'd been possessed. Then he looked at her and couldn't think of anything other than finding a way to spend more time with her.

She smoothed her hair, which had blown wild in the wind outside. Her cheeks were pink from the chilled air, the smattering of freckles standing out on her pert nose. He had to resist the urge to lean over and kiss her. Her green eyes held his, a flash of uncertainty blinking in their depths. She took a deep breath. Little did she know that every time she did that, her shirt stretched tighter across her breasts and all he could think about is what it would feel like to touch her. The wind gusted around outside, leaves dancing in the air. He started his truck and turned the heat on to drive the chill out.

Marley finally answered. "Okay, dinner. What are we celebrating?"

"That you helped me deal with something I was clueless about it. Now it's done. By the end of next week, I'll have the new furniture delivered. A little work inside will have the place ready to roll after I take care of the painting and a few other repairs outside." He shifted into gear and started driving.

"I guess I didn't think it was that big of a deal. All I did was ask the salesperson a few questions and follow him around," she said with a chuckle.

"This part just isn't my thing. Put me to work on construction or some other project, but don't ask me to decide on furniture or design a website." He paused and glanced at her when he stopped at a light. "For me, your help means a lot. I want the lodge up and running by Christmas. Much as I'd somehow convinced myself I could do it all by myself, clearly I can't. So thank you."

Marley flushed and looked away. "Well, you're welcome," she said softly. She turned back to him, her green eyes bright. "People are going to be so excited about the lodge opening again. I don't think you really understand how much it will mean around town."

Gage was mesmerized by her eyes. He couldn't look away. Though he sensed her uncertainty, when she spoke, it was with meaning and without artifice. Her simple statement about the lodge tugged at him. And damned if he knew why. He stared at her for so long, a car honked behind him, finally snapping him out of his trance. His body hummed at her nearness. He cleared his throat and tore his eyes from hers, shifting back into gear and zipping through the intersection and onto the exit for Sterling Highway, the sole highway that led to Diamond Creek and further down the peninsula to a few other small towns until it ended in Homer, Alaska—otherwise known as the end of the road, which it was, literally.

The highway hugged the coastline on the western side of the Kenai Peninsula, rolling past vistas of snow-capped mountains on the other side of the inlet. The sun was dipping in the sky as he drove south, a path of shimmering gold and pink falling on the water as they drove. An eagle flew low along the shoreline, a pair of moose stood tall in a field of faded fireweed. Gage remembered this drive when he was a little boy. His clearest memory was when his parents were moving them to Washington. He recalled driving away in the summer and watching the caravan of campers heading into Alaska. He remembered that he hadn't really understood they were moving away and that it would mean he wouldn't be in this place he loved so.

Now, so many years later, he felt like he was home again. Yet, he wasn't the boy he once was. The drive to Diamond Creek was mostly quiet. Gage had quickly grown to appreciate two things about Marley—when she chose to talk, it was usually interesting, and she was completely comfortable with quiet. He wanted to know more about her—what it was like to grow up in Diamond Creek, why she left, why she came back, how did she become a computer programmer, what made her tick, where was her favorite hiking trail, and her favorite food.

As he began to add to the list of questions he wanted Marley to answer, it occurred to him that he was breaking all of his own rules with her. He'd returned from his last mission, buried his best friend, and walked into a desk job on the base. A job he thought would help him erase the desolate sense he felt inside. It only made him feel worse. Becoming a Navy SEAL was an experience of precision and intense, grueling effort. Years of that layered onto the experience of war made sitting at a desk next to impossible.

When Gram died and her attorney had contacted him and his siblings to review the will, he'd known that afternoon what he would do. Deep in his grief because they all loved Gram, he'd made plans. He was the oldest of his siblings at thirty-four. The twins came next, Garrett and Becca at thirty-two. Garrett was brainy and buttoned-up, a high-flying lawyer in Seattle. His twin sister, Becca, was so similar and so different at once. She was also a lawyer, but a poorly paid public prosecutor who specialized in cases involving victims of abuse.

Next came Sawyer at thirty who'd followed Gage onto the path of becoming a Navy SEAL and was currently in the thick of his career, often out of contact on confidential missions. Last but definitely not least was Jessa at twenty-eight. Jessa was the free spirit in the family and was currently doing freelance work building artsy furniture that she sold for ridiculously high prices. Jessa had been on his case about making sure to set up a website and insisting he get help with decorating the lodge. She'd threatened to come up and do it herself, which had spurred him into action. He missed his family, but his hope was that once he got Last Frontier Lodge up and running, they'd come visit often. Of his siblings, he was the only one who had clear memories of when they lived here. His goal was to have the place ready for Christmas and have the whole family here. Though his family knew he had the skills to do what needed to be done, he didn't think they quite recognized the depth of his intention.

This was a dream he needed to recapture. Staring down the loss of his best friend and trying to pull the pieces of his life together made him want the peace he recalled from Alaska. It was the first thing he'd wanted in a long time. When Gram died and left him the primary owner of the lodge, he knew if he ever had a chance to find peace again, he might be able to find it here in Diamond Creek.

Marley…she was something he hadn't anticipated. She bumped against the boundaries he'd put in place. But for the moment, he was trying to convince himself he could have it both ways.

When they reached Diamond Creek and he came to one of the few stoplights in town, he looked over at her. "Any favorites?"

"Favorite what?"

"Favorite restaurants."

Her wide smile reached in and grabbed his heart. He didn't know why that made her smile, but he didn't care. Her smile was like rain to the parched soil of his soul.

"Oh, let's go to Diamond Creek Brewery. It's one of my favorites. Have you been there?"

"I've barely left the lodge since I've been here. I'm familiar with the grocery store and the hardware store, but definitely not Diamond Creek Brewery. Tell me where to go."

Marley gave him directions and in minutes, he pulled up outside an old plane hangar. The only indication it wasn't just a plane hangar was the brightly painted sign and the well-lit parking lot. He glanced over at her. "Um, this is a plane hangar, not a restaurant."

She grinned and his heart swelled. "It might be a plane hangar, but there's a restaurant inside. Come on," she said, climbing out his truck and grabbing her purse.

Gage followed her inside and looked around. Though the space was technically a plane hangar, it was a far cry from its original purpose inside. The back end of the cavernous space held an actual beer brewery, the brewing equipment behind a three-quarters high brick wall. The wide-open space above had elaborate model planes hanging from the ceiling, reminiscent of the many small planes used throughout Alaska for travel. Windows had been added to the hangar walls and offered the view of a marshy field with Kachemak Bay and the mountains in the distance. Booths lined the walls with tables scattered in the middle. It was clear the brewery was popular with people filling most tables, the booths and the bar. Artistic fabric wall hangings and colorful rugs under the tables softened the noise in the space.

They had to wait a few minutes for a booth to open up. Gage quickly realized being with Marley meant he'd have to get through introductions. Given that she'd grown up here, in the brief time they waited, she was greeted by at least five different people. When they sat down, a woman with wild brown curls and a bright smile approached their booth.

"Marley! I heard you moved back. How's it going?"

Marley stood and gave a quick hug to the woman and sat back down. The woman instantly turned her gaze to Gage, not bothering to hide her curiosity. "And who might this be?" she asked.

"Gage Hamilton," Marley replied. "Gage, this is Susie," she continued, gesturing to Susie. "She was a little ahead of me in school, but our moms used to take turns babysitting. Susie thought I was a book nerd..."

Susie interjected with a grin, her smile infectious. "You were and are!"

Marley grinned and continued. "Susie,

this is Gage. He's reopening Last Frontier Lodge."

Gage instantly got a sense of what Marley meant when she said people would be happy to hear he was opening the old ski lodge. Susie's eyes widened and she clapped her hands, her brown curls bouncing.

"Really? Oh, this is awesome! So how did you end up with the lodge and when will it be open?"

After Gage explained his grandparents had owned it and he'd been born in Diamond Creek, Susie's eyed him thoughtfully.

"How come I don't know you?" she asked.

Marley burst out laughing. "Susie, you don't know everyone even if you like to think you do. Plus, he moved away when we were really little."

Susie shrugged and grinned. "Whatever. Well, I'll be spreading the word about Last Frontier Lodge, so you'd better stay on schedule."

"I'll do my best," he replied.

Susie glanced to Marley. "Are the rumors true then, you're here to stay?"

Marley nodded quickly. "All true." Her voice was bright, but her eyes were guarded.

Gage couldn't help but wonder what lay behind that.

Marley continued. "Didn't I hear that you got married and had a baby?"

Susie grinned and nodded, her curls bouncing. "You heard right. I still can't believe it myself. I married Jared Winters and little Patrick came along just last year. I'm not sure if you know Jared and his brothers. They moved here about five years ago and started a guide business."

Marley shook her head. The conversation continued between them while Gage glanced around the restaurant. Susie turned to leave, waving as she went. Their waitress arrived seconds later. Gage discovered the brewery's choices of beer were extensive, along with a varied menu. After settling on a beer and pizza, he leaned back. His memories of Alaska were limited to his time at the ski lodge. He didn't remember if Diamond Creek had any restaurants whatsoever, but he was pleased to find the brewery could have easily held its own in a place such as Bellingham or Seattle.

Dinner passed pleasantly. The more time Gage spent with Marley, the more he enjoyed her. The constant hum of attraction to her was distracting. He was learning just how convenient tables were when he was with Marley since they hid the almost-constant bulge in his pants. She filled him in on the highlights of her childhood and what led her to Seattle. She clearly loved her work, becoming animated when she discussed projects she'd worked on, and her hopes to keep herself afloat with freelance work as an app developer. The only hiccup was when he asked her what led her to return to Diamond Creek. Her eyes shuttered, and there was a long moment of silence. Though he was still getting to know her, he knew his innocent question had rattled her.

"I just wanted to come home," she finally said with a shrug. Her green eyes were guarded. She took a deep breath and turned the focus to him. "So what about you? I mean, I know you inherited the lodge and all with your siblings, but not everyone would drop their life and move to Alaska like you have. What were you doing before?" she asked.

Gage took a long breath, wondering how to explain the events that led him on the long road back to Diamond Creek. Rather than skirting the truth, he elected to keep it bare bones. "I enlisted in the Navy straight out of college. I trained to become a Navy SEAL and that became my life. To keep it brief, after years of missions, it was time to take a break. It was hard to readjust to civilian life when I got back. Then Gram died and we got the lodge, so I decided to take a chance. When I was little, I dreamed about coming back. Some of the best memories I have are from Alaska. So here I am."

Gage left out the details too painful to consider—Matt's death in Iraq after his helicopter was shot down, having to fly back in a military plane with what was left of Matt's body, and wonder why random luck left him alive and Matt who had a wife and daughter dead. With a force of will, he shoved those thoughts away and looked across the table at Marley with her forest green eyes, scattered freckles, auburn hair he wanted to run his hands through, and full lips he wanted to taste.

If Marley was aware of the inner turmoil he'd experienced trying to skate across the surface of the events that brought him here, she didn't let on. She kept the conversation light and circled back to planning for the lodge, telling him she thought she could have his website up and ready by tomorrow if he wanted.

"Tomorrow? Why would I need it up tomorrow? It's two months to December."

Marley tilted her head and wrinkled her pert nose, which was like flicking a switch in his body. The attraction buzzing in his veins amped up.

"You need a website sooner rather than later, so people will find out Last Frontier Lodge exists and will be open again. It'll take some legwork, but you should look into advertising options, so you can make it visible online. People could start making reservations now. If you're worried about what to post, I can set it up for you to have a blog where you post updates on your progress. People love stuff like that."

Gage watched her and made an instant decision. "I'm hiring you," he said bluntly.

"Huh? I already told you the website is no big deal."

"I need more than that. I can't do this stuff you're talking about. I get it, I understand it needs to happen, but advertising, writing updates on a blog, none of that will happen if it's left to me. Please say you'll do it. You told me you're trying to figure out the work thing. While you're doing that, you can help me get this side of things worked out. I'll do the rest."

As soon as the words left his mouth, Gage realized he was desperate for her to say yes. Not only did he genuinely need the kind of help she could offer, he wanted any chance he could get to spend more time with her. When Marley looked hesitant, he begged. "Please. Look at me. Can you see me doing this stuff? Not my thing. Please help. I have money from Gram to put into getting the lodge going again. You'll be our first employee. And it's perfect because I'm clueless in this area, so you'll be your own boss."

Marley bit her lip, and he couldn't look away. She finally nodded, by which point his mind had wandered onto remembering just how good her lips tasted. When his brain caught up to her nod, he couldn't help his grin. Her yes meant that many more opportunities to be near her. *Are you out of your mind?* The rational side of his brain was seriously wondering what had gotten into him. At the moment, he didn't bother to entertain it.

"Okay. I'll do it, but…" She held a finger up. "…you'd better get cracking on the repairs because I'm going to be announcing all over the place that the lodge will be open by Christmas because that's what you said you wanted."

Gage nodded firmly. "You have my word."

CHAPTER 6

*M*arley walked ahead of Gage into her small cabin. She'd offered to show him what she'd been working on for his website. It was mostly ready to go, other than adding the blog she'd suggested. She'd wondered throughout the short drive home if she'd been crazy to agree to work for Gage. The work part wouldn't be too difficult, but spending too much time around him would likely fluster her beyond comprehension. All day, she'd been sneaking glances at him. His jeans rode low on his hips. When he moved, she saw flashes of his rock-hard abs. She almost lost herself in his eyes when she looked at him. A low charge hummed through her body, desire sliding through her veins at every look and passing touch.

When they entered her cabin, she flicked on a lamp by the door. It cast a soft circle of light. The common area downstairs was an open kitchen into living room area with floor to ceiling windows that came to a peak at the top. A small bathroom and laundry area was off of the kitchen. The upstairs consisted of two bedrooms and a bathroom. She hung her jacket and kicked her shoes off, Gage following suit. Her pulse pounding, Marley walked toward the small desk to the side of the living room. Before she reached it, Gage said her name, his voice gruff in the quiet space.

She turned to find him right behind her. His smoky gaze locked with hers. His sculpted features were cast in shadow. His lips quirked when he took a step closer, coming within inches of her. His body emanated heat. Her breath caught. Her pulse pounded, heat gathering inside, a slow burn in her belly. Awareness prickled across her skin.

Gage opened his mouth as if to say something and then shook his head sharply. He swore under his breath and next thing she knew, his lips were on hers. She tumbled headlong into the cauldron of desire swirling around them. She hadn't known her body felt so desolate without Gage's touch, but she drank in his touch as if she'd been parched. He kissed slowly and deeply, his tongue delving in to meet hers, pulling back to trace her lips, catching her bottom lip in his teeth and tugging lightly before trailing his lips down her neck in a path of fire.

Marley's body gloried everywhere he touched her. He tugged her roughly against his body. The feel of his hard muscles was a heaven she couldn't have imagined. They were standing beside the back of the couch. Gage turned and rested his hips against it, pulling her into the cradle of his thighs. She felt surrounded by strength, warmth, heat, and an encompassing passion she couldn't deny.

His palms slid under the back of her shirt, warm and strong, the calloused surface sending sparks across her skin. He deftly unhooked her bra and slipped his hands around to cup her breasts. She groaned into his mouth at the feel of his touch. She hadn't known how much she'd missed being touched. She couldn't have imagined that anyone could make her feel the way Gage did. She was hot, achy and frantic for more. When he pulled her shirt up over her head, she sighed in relief when it fell to the floor and his lips closed around a nipple.

Burning for more, she shoved his shirt up. He reached behind his neck and in one motion tugged his shirt off, tossing it behind him. She groaned when her body came against his, the feel of his skin electric. His hands were everywhere, his knee shifted between her thighs. With every motion of the rough denim against her center, pleasure streaked through her. His name came out in a broken gasp when he rolled her taut nipples between his fingers. She pleaded for more, a small shriek escaping when he finally closed his mouth around a nipple again after teasing her to the point of madness. She was wound so tight inside, she didn't recognize herself.

Her hips shifted restlessly against his leg as she raced toward a release she didn't know if she could survive without. Gage suddenly paused, coming still. He said her name, his gravelly voice sending shivers through her. She opened her eyes to find his smoky, lightning gray gaze on her.

She tried to rein her mind in and force herself to focus, but the buzz of desire was so strong, she could barely manage. She shook her head. "What?"

"You have to know, I don't want to stop," he said, his voice strained. He swallowed and took a slow breath. "But I don't know if this is what you want. I like you. I don't want things to get weird if this goes too far, too fast."

Reality started to intrude in her mind. Gage's mere existence muddied her thoughts and shoved reason out of the way. Gage was far more experienced than she was and likely meant for this to be nothing more than a fling. She didn't even know if she could handle a fling. Meanwhile, her body screamed for her to ignore reason. She looked into his eyes and realized she wanted him with a ferocity she'd never wanted anyone. But she was far from knowing him well enough to know what he wanted and wasn't so sure she knew what she wanted. Other than him. Inside of her. *Now.*

"I, uh, don't know. I guess. This, um, thing between us is kind of...a lot."

Her body moved of its own accord, her hips shifting against his thigh again. Her face was afire, hot and flushed. Gage's eyes darkened and flicked down to her breasts. She was bare in front of him, her nipples glistening in the lamplight, her breasts heavy with want for more of his touch. She could feel his arousal against her leg—hard, thick, and hot.

Gage's eyes landed on hers again. "We're in agreement there. This is *a lot*." He paused. His hands had fallen to rest on her hips. He ran them up her sides, his thumbs coasting across the soft curve of her belly, and brought them up to curl around her breasts again. "I can't seem to keep my hands off of you. So if you want this to stop, say the word. Now."

Marley stared at him through the soft light, his smoky gaze locked with hers. She tried to think clearly, but need pounded through her. In a flash, she decided she would follow what her body wanted. She hadn't been intimate with anyone in years, and had never even come close to feeling what she felt with Gage. She didn't want to miss the chance to taste more, even if she had to untangle her feelings later. "I don't want to stop," she said softly.

He inhaled sharply, his eyes darkening. He lifted a hand and stroked it through her hair, his palm cupping the back of her head. Hot shivers raced through her. His eyes fell closed as he brought his mouth to hers again. She tumbled into a hot, wild kiss that went on and on and on. Gage's hands roamed over her body—a palm sliding down her back in a delicious caress, a hand cupping her breast, softly thumbing her nipple, both hands curling around her bottom and dragging her closer to him.

She was awash in a tumult of sensation. He tugged her close against his hard chest. The contrast of his hardness against her soft curves was intoxicating. She gasped in his mouth when his knee shifted between her legs, pressing against the center of her desire. Sensation sharpened within, gathering pressure. Desire danced and sizzled in her veins. The remainder of their clothing was torn off. In a blur, she found herself standing before him, bare save her purple silk panties. Gage was seated on the couch, his arousal evident. His body took her breath away. Every inch was hard muscle, honed to perfection. His eyes were on her, his gaze like fire as he looked over her body. He reached his hands up, resting them on her hips and tugged her forward.

He looked up, and she watched as he dragged a hand across her belly and down. She was drenched in desire, the silk wet. He stroked his thumb across her clit through the silk. Already ragged, her breath fell out in a gasp. He hooked a finger over the edge of her panties and tugged them down. She kicked them away as they fell around her ankles.

"Beautiful…"

Marley couldn't quite believe he thought that, but his eyes were reverent as they coasted over her. Tossed in the wake of passion, she couldn't form a reply. Before she knew what was happening, Gage tugged her hips closer and brought his mouth to her. Hot, wet strokes of his tongue, his fingers delving inside her channel, plunging in and out in a slow rhythm. She tumbled so far, so fast, her climax took her by surprise, washing over her in a crashing wave. Her knees buckled. Gage's strong arm latched around her, holding her steady while he stayed with her as she shuddered.

His fingers slid out of her, his mouth slowly moving away when she finally stilled. Dazed, she met his eyes. Holding her gaze, he stood and lifted her in his arms.

"Bedroom?" he asked.

Hardly able to form a thought, she gestured weakly to the stairs. He moved swiftly, following the direction of her gesture to the top of the stairs. He shouldered through the door to her bedroom. Her brain had started to function, though barely, by the time he set her on the bed. She reached to the nightstand and switched on the lamp. He stood beside the bed, his body a sculpted work of art. Though she'd just had the most earth-shattering orgasm she'd ever experienced, the sight of his body inflamed her. His gaze traveled over her, his eyes dark. She didn't know when he'd grabbed a condom, but he had one in hand. He tore the package with his teeth and rolled it on, his eyes pinned to her the entire time. She couldn't have looked away if her life depended on it. As it was, she was fairly certain her body couldn't make it past this moment without the feel of him inside of her.

She trembled with want as he moved toward her. The bed dipped when he rested on a knee, the heat of his body moving over hers in blur. She felt the tip of his cock at her entrance. His elbows bracketed her face. He brushed her tangled hair off her forehead, his eyes dark and intent. The air around them felt alive—vibrating with passion. She shifted restlessly under him, desperate to feel him inside of her. She should have known he'd maintain control and drive her further into the fire that consumed her. He proceeded to feather kisses across her face, down her neck and over her breasts. All the while, he nudged at her entrance in subtle strokes.

Unable to tolerate the want coiling inside of her, she scored his back when she dragged her nails down and grabbed his hips, arching into him. He swore and surged into her in one deep thrust, filling her completely. Though she wasn't a virgin, years without sex left her tight. Gage was, of course, well-endowed. She gasped at the feel of him inside, stretching her. He held still for a long moment, and then began to move. She may have broken his discipline long enough to get him inside of her, but he found it again and proceeded to drive her wild with slow strokes.

Feverish with desire, she tumbled back into the web around them. She danced on the delicious edge of another orgasm, the pressure building and building until she shattered and flew apart. Only then did he alter his pace, his hips drumming into hers, his back arching as he shuddered against her. In the aftermath, he fell to her side, still inside of her. They lay still in the quiet room—the only sound their ragged breathing.

As Marley came back to herself, she felt suddenly self-conscious. She'd wanted this like she'd never wanted anything before. But she couldn't have known she'd lose herself in it. She figured Gage was accustomed to making women fall apart in his arms. She braved a glance at him and found his gray eyes closed, his lashes dark against his cheeks. His chest rose and fell with his breath. As she looked at him, he opened his eyes. She flushed, but she managed not to look away. He lifted a hand and cupped her cheek before bringing his lips to hers briefly. Without a word, he shifted his hips away from hers and rolled to stand. He strode to the bathroom adjacent to her bedroom. She heard a rustle and the water running before he returned. She assumed he'd disposed of his condom.

Entirely unselfconscious about his body, he walked to the bed and lifted the covers, gesturing for her to move. Uncertain what he meant to do, she rolled out of the way. He climbed in bed beside her and tucked the quilt around them both, pulling her against his chest. His palm was warm on her back as he stroked in slow circles, the rough skin sending tiny shivers through her. She couldn't help the sense of comfort that stole over her—unfamiliar and yet a feeling she craved.

Gage's chest rumbled when he spoke. "Unless you tell me I can't stay here, I wasn't planning on leaving."

Marley lifted her head. His eyes met hers, the tiniest glimmer of uncertainty flaring in their depths. She took a breath. "I wasn't planning to ask you to leave," she said softly.

"Well, that's settled then."

His voice was gruff, the corner of his mouth kicked up. She couldn't help her smile. He reached behind her and switched off the lamp. Resting her head on his shoulder, she looked out the window that faced the forest. Stars were bright in the dark sky. A sliver of the moon sat above the mountains across the bay. She fell asleep, feeling sated, safe and warm. For the first time in months, it didn't cross her mind to check the locks.

CHAPTER 7

Gage walked across the roof to the area where he'd left some extra shingles. He'd spent most of the morning replacing torn and missing shingles on the lodge's interconnected rooftops. For the most part, the roof had held up well, but long winters, windstorms and ice had left a few damaged areas. He was finishing up the last repair. He grabbed the shingles and strode back to where he was working. He quickly pried up the torn shingle and replaced it with a new section. After applying sealant and nailing it in place, he hefted the backpack he'd used to carry his tools and tossed it over his shoulders. The roof had a slight slope to it, but it was easy enough to walk around. He paused by the chimney in the center of the main portion of the lodge and admired the view. Kachemak Bay sat quietly under the sun, the water calm today. The snowy mountains were bright against the blue sky. From here, he could see beyond the bay into Cook Inlet, Mount Augustine rising in the waters in the distance. The air was brisk, the scent of wood smoke drifting from someone's woodstove.

He instantly wondered if it was Marley's. It had been two days since she'd knocked the axis of his world sideways. Before he'd been skin to skin with her, he'd become quite familiar with the depth of his lust for her. But he couldn't have known what it would feel like to *be* with her. He'd walked in thinking he could control the situation. Instead, he'd come out on the other side wondering how to catch hold of the reins again. Marley affected him like no woman had ever affected him. Her complete lack of artifice combined with her utter abandonment into the passion that burned like a brushfire between them was intoxicating. He turned and walked to the edge of the roof, quickly climbing down the ladder. The sun was still high in the sky, but it was early afternoon, which meant he only had a few hours of good daylight left to add another coat of paint on one of the buildings.

Hours later, he leaned against the steel table that ran through the center of the main kitchen at the lodge. As a boy, he recalled this room as a bustle of activity from dawn until late at night. He'd made his way through stacks of faded cards with phone numbers from the old staff at the lodge. Though it had been many years since any of them would have worked here, Gage figured it was worth a shot to do some reconnaissance to find out if any former employees were still in town. The further he got into the work of his dream to reopen the lodge, the more he realized he needed help, lots of help.

His vision of reopening the lodge was turning out to be rather vague. He'd convinced himself he'd do the hard work of repairs and the lodge would magically open. Thanks to Marley, he had help with the online side of things, but he needed a functioning restaurant, staff to handle the hotel guests, and staff on the slopes. The coffee maker beeped, and he strode over and poured a cup. He liked his coffee strong and black—no frills. He walked from the kitchen into the office and started perusing the list of names he'd found.

"Hello?"

He whirled around in his chair to find an older man standing in the doorway. The man was tall, lean and weathered. Gage thought he was familiar, but he couldn't place him.

"Hi there, can I help you?" Gage asked.

The man removed the faded baseball cap he wore and eyed Gage. "Gage Hamilton?"

Gage nodded slowly. "That's me."

The man's blue eyes crinkled at the corners with a smile that instantly shifted to a chuckle. "Well, well. I heard from the guys at the hardware store you were up here doing all kinds of work. I'm guessing you don't remember me."

Gage eyed the man. "You look familiar, but if you know who I am, then you know I haven't been here in about twenty years. I'm not up to speed on who's who. Care to refresh my memory?"

The man stepped into the room. Gage stood to meet him, reaching out to shake his hand. "Don Peters. I worked for your grandparents for years, mostly running the lifts and doing slope work, but I helped out on the grounds during the rest of the year. My wife ran the kitchen during ski season."

Gage's memory clicked. "Oh yes! I remember you now. Good to see you. Have a seat," he said, gesturing for Don to sit in one of the chairs at the table nearby.

He grabbed his cup of coffee and followed him over. "Would you like some coffee? Can't say I can even come close to what your wife used to do around here, but I can make coffee."

Don shook his head. "No thanks. Just thought I'd drop in and take a look around." His eyes traveled around the sparsely furnished office and through the door into the empty restaurant. When his eyes made it back around the room to Gage's, they held a hint of sadness. "Damn, it's been a long time. Hard to see this place empty."

Don shifted in his chair. Gage experienced a pang, recognizing that while he'd only known this man in passing when he was young, Don had been a fixture at the ski lodge. Gage remembered Don's wife, Sandy, well. He'd spent many a snowy afternoon running in and out of the kitchen looking for whatever scraps of food Sandy would provide. She often made them sandwiches for lunch and snuck him bits and pieces of fancier dishes on big nights at the lodge. His memory was of a warm, soft woman, her hair always worn in a braid that swung over her shoulder, her bright brown eyes kind and smiling.

"I remember your wife. She was always feeding me and my brothers and sisters. Sandy, right?"

The sadness in Don's eyes sharpened, but he didn't look away. He nodded brusquely. "Sandy wanted to feed the world, and she mostly did around here in Diamond Creek. She loved you kids. She, uh, passed away three years ago. Pancreatic cancer. By the time they found it, it was too late. Though we learned not many people survive that kind of cancer. I'm just glad she didn't have a lot of pain." Don paused. "I miss her every day," he said plainly. "She'd have been beside herself to know you were opening this place again. Had to come see for myself."

Gage's heart tightened, a flash of sadness piercing him. Though Sandy was but a memory for him, she was a part of what he'd loved at the lodge—she'd made everyone feel welcome. He met Don's eyes and wanted to turn back time. Time was both a blessing and a curse. Time passed and pain eased. But one could never go back, so when you lost someone you loved, you had to accept the finality of it. He was pleased to know Sandy would have been happy about the lodge opening again. He only hoped he could do it justice. He took a breath. "I'm so sorry to hear about your wife. I, uh, wish I'd had a chance to see her again. I may have been away for a long time, but I remember her well. She was funny and nice and always took care of us kids."

Don nodded slowly, his smile soft and worn. "Sandy was that kind of woman. If you spent much time with her, she was hard to forget, so thank you for that. But I'm okay. I miss her, but she'd give me all kinds of hell if I moped around too much, so I try to live the way she'd want me to. That's what got me up here today. Boy, if she were still with us, she'd have been pounding down your door. So what's the plan?"

"Well, I had a great plan and I thought it was really simple. When Gram died, I inherited this place with my brothers and sisters. I've got the largest share and seem to be the only one who missed this place like crazy. So, I came up here to reopen it. I thought all I'd need to do was take care of a few repairs and off we'd go." He sighed and ran a hand through his hair. "I forgot the hard part—like running the restaurant, finding staff to help out on the slopes, that kind of thing. I found a little help for the website though. Marley Adams offered to help with that, which is a damn good thing because I have no clue about that. My sisters keep saying I had to get a website, but without Marley, I don't think it would happen."

Saying Marley's name conjured her in Gage's mind. His body instantly tightened. He had to force his thoughts off of her and back to Don.

Don grinned. "Marley Adams, huh? She's a good kid. Her parents are good friends of ours. I mean, mine. She just moved back to town after that scare in Seattle. Her parents are tickled pink, and I'm glad to hear she's helping you out. She needs something to do. That brain of hers never stops."

Gage couldn't help it. His mind got hung up on the "scare in Seattle" that Don mentioned. It brought back a memory from the other night when he asked her why she moved back to Diamond Creek. She'd answered, but her answer had been vague and her eyes had been guarded. "I ran into her when she was hiking up here. I gathered she only moved back recently, but what happened?"

Don didn't seem to mind Gage's question and appeared oblivious to the depth of Gage's curiosity. "She walked into her apartment being robbed in Seattle. Her father told me she got lucky to come away with only a few bruises. Guy whipped her good with his gun and then stripped her place. Her parents have wanted her back home for years. She's smart as a whip and could probably run circles around those city tech guys, but she's a Diamond Creek girl through and through. I'm glad to know you met her. Though I haven't seen you in years, you were always a good boy. She could use a friend," Don said gruffly.

Gage barely heard a word Don said past the details of the robbery. Fury rushed through him so fast he had to force himself to breath slowly. Fortunately, he was an expert at staying stone cold on the outside no matter how he felt inside. Knowing that someone hurt Marley like that just to steal from her made him sick with anger. His mind locked on the wish to personally find and destroy the man who hurt her. On the heels of that anger came an intense wave of protectiveness.

Don cleared his throat. Gage realized he'd gone quiet. He wasn't concerned the turmoil he felt inside had shown, but he had some manners. He met Don's eyes again. "That shouldn't happen to anyone. I'm glad she's okay. Do you know if they caught whoever did it?"

Don shrugged. "Far as I know, they haven't. It's only been a few months. She moved back about a month ago."

Gage nodded slowly. "Well, good thing she's back. Can't imagine something like that happening around here."

Don shook his head. "Definitely not. You probably didn't realize it, but you got yourself a hot shot computer programmer getting your website going. Marley'll do a good job for you," he said, grinning proudly.

Gage kept his focus firmly on the present. He knew if he let himself think too much about what Don told him, his mind would go in circles. He shifted the topic off Marley. "Speaking of help, any suggestions on who I could hire here? I'd like to have the lodge open by the holidays. I'm not saying that's what you're looking for, but if you want your old job back, it's yours. I could use any help you're willing to give."

Don's eyes twinkled. "Well, damn. I wasn't expecting that. I gotta say, I figured you were up here doing your own thing. I wasn't so sure you meant to get this place up and running by Christmas."

Gage nodded firmly. "I'm starting to wonder if I'm crazy, but that's what I want. I figure I'd better. I told Marley I hoped to have it open by Christmas and now she tells me she's posted it online."

Don chuckled before his eyes sobered. "I wasn't looking for work, but of all the jobs I did, I loved working at the lodge the best. I'd be happy to help out. I'm not as young as I used to be, but I'm not too old either. Your grandfather hired me on when I was a skinny, smartass teenager. Tell me when and I'll be here. Nothing would make Sandy happier than this place being open again. Not to mention, it'll give me something to do."

Gage grinned and stuck his hand out for another shake. "You just made my day. I was about to sit down and go through the list of names I found in Gram's desk and see if I could figure out if any of her old staff were still around. Having you here to help me figure things out makes me feel like we might be able to pull this off."

Don shook his hand vigorously. "We're gonna make it fun." His eyes sobered and he glanced around. "I can help with getting the lifts up and going and all the outside stuff, but I'm not your guy for the kitchen and reception."

"Any suggestions on who I can call?"

"I'll start by asking my daughter. She was tied to her mama's hip in the kitchen. She might not be up for it, but she can give us some ideas on who would be."

Gage nodded firmly. "Perfect. Back to you, when do you want to start?"

Don shrugged. "Tell me when you need me. I haven't worked much since Sandy passed away. Odd jobs here and there, but nothing else."

"Tomorrow?" Gage asked hopefully.

Don laughed and stood, putting his baseball cap on as he did. "Tomorrow it is."

Gage walked him outside and gave him a brief tour of the work he'd done already on the exterior. Don left with promises to return tomorrow and assess the condition of the slopes. Gage walked down the driveway after Don left and eyed the sign again. He'd put in entirely new posts yesterday and repainted the lettering on the sign. Last Frontier Lodge was legible now. He turned and looked down the hill toward Marley's cabin, its bright red roof peeking out through the spruce forest.

The fury he'd tamped down and held in washed over him in a wave. He knew well that life wasn't fair. He'd learned that lesson time and again. But to think Marley—sweet, sexy, Marley who'd somehow found a way to crawl through his defenses and flash a ray of sunshine inside his battened down heart —had been attacked and robbed. He could hardly stand to think it. He closed his eyes and took a breath—the cold, bracing autumn air rushing through him. He didn't know how, but he'd find a way to make sure she never got hurt like that again.

CHAPTER 8

$\mathcal{M}$arley stood up from the couch where she'd been planted for most of the morning, deep into work on one of her app projects. She'd sent it out for beta testing to a few trusted contacts before switching over to post an update on the lodge's website. Gage had grumbled, but he'd allowed her to take photographs of the repairs he'd finished on the lodge for the purpose of posting them on the blog. She knew they needed to raise the profile of the lodge online, and she hoped using the blog to post cute updates would stir interest. True to his word, Gage was clueless in the online world. She'd been childishly pleased he went along with her plan for the photos. Once she finished posting the photos, she closed her laptop and forced herself to get off the couch. The cabin had a slice of a view of Kachemak Bay through a gap in the trees. The water sparkled in the sun, wind ruffling the surface. She walked to the door at the side of the kitchen and out onto the deck, which wrapped around the cabin.

Autumn was almost gone. She expected it to snow any day now. Every morning, the snow fell lower on the mountains across the bay. Living close to the ski lodge meant living fairly high up in the foothills that encircled Diamond Creek. Downtown Diamond Creek was a descent of over one thousand feet down to sea level. The hills around town could have a foot of snow, while downtown by the ocean may only have a few inches. A bracing wind blew through the trees. She breathed deep, invigorated by the sharp, cold air.

She turned and looked up toward the ski lodge. The buildings were visible above the treetops. In the distance, she saw a man on a ladder resting against the side of the main lodge. Though all she could see was a silhouette, she knew it must be Gage. Her breath caught and her pulse raced. The other night with Gage had taken her to a place she'd never been, and she could hardly stop thinking about him. She hadn't seen him for two days afterwards by virtue of her mother cajoling her into a trip to Anchorage for shopping. She'd been somewhat relieved because she could barely behave normally around him, and thought perhaps a day or two away would set her head straight and get her hormones under control.

No such luck. Gage had texted and called both days. While his queries had mostly been mundane, he sent her heart wild when he commented that he hoped she wasn't avoiding him. His voice had become gruff when he said this. Marley had squeezed the phone in her hand and forced herself to keep a straight face with her mother driving in the car beside her. She wasn't avoiding him, but she also didn't know what to do with her feelings. He'd blown her mind and body the other night. Any free moment, her mind wandered to thoughts of him. She wanted to ask him what he wanted, but she didn't quite dare. She was afraid all he wanted was to take advantage of the chemistry that crackled like a

livewire between them. It was discombobu-
lating that a tiny corner of her heart wanted
something more.

Replaying the moment in her mind, she
flushed. Another gust of wind coasted
through the trees, cooling her heated skin.
With a whirl, Marley turned and went inside, snatching her purse and climbing in
her car. An old friend had called her this
morning about meeting for lunch. She
quickly texted to confirm she was on her
way. Beyond wanting to reconnect with
friends, she needed something to get her
mind off of Gage. She'd never experienced
the way she felt with him and didn't like
how out of control it made her feel.

A short drive later, Marley walked into
Glacier Pizza, one of her old favorites. The
restaurant remained just as she recalled. A
brick oven stove sat center stage with an
open kitchen surrounding it. A counter
with stools encircled the kitchen, and
booths lined the walls. The restaurant was
decorated almost as an afterthought with
photos from locals and tourists adorning
the walls. Various license plates from all
over the country hung on a back wall.

She glanced around, her eyes landing on

her friend, Ginger Sanders. Ginger was one of her oldest friends. They'd grown up together in the small world of Diamond Creek and stayed tight all through college. Marley had missed her dearly the entire time she was in Seattle. Ginger hadn't noticed her yet and was busy perusing the menu. Marley strode over to the booth and tapped Ginger on the shoulder. Ginger's head snapped up, and she squealed. With a leap, she stood and hugged Marley tight.

"It's so good to see you!" Ginger stepped back, brushing her hair out of her face. "I hate that you've been here over a month, and I've been out of town the whole time. How are you?"

Marley swallowed at the sudden tightness in her throat. No matter how long it was between when they talked, it was as if no time had passed. She felt instantly comfortable. She met Ginger's blue gaze and tears spilled down her cheeks. Being home for more than a visit was bringing up feelings she hadn't known she'd buried. A decade away in Seattle, so often feeling a step out of rhythm with everyone there and never quite feeling like she belonged, had forced her to tuck her feelings away.

Even when she visited Diamond Creek, she'd had to keep it light, reminding herself why she'd moved away—to make something of herself. Ginger's bright blue eyes and her ever-present warmth and acceptance were merely one thing she'd missed dearly.

Ginger tugged Marley close again for another hug. When she stepped back this time, her eyes glistened. "Sit down and tell me everything," she said, waving Marley into the booth.

Marley pulled her jacket off and sat down, tucking her jacket and purse to her side on the seat. She met Ginger's eyes. "I can't tell you how good it is to see you. I didn't think it would make me cry though," she said with a wry smile.

Ginger giggled. "Hey, I'd have missed me that much too."

Marley grinned and took a sip of the water waiting for her on the table. "So, what training kept you away for a whole month?"

"I was finishing up the advanced portion of my internship, so I can officially call myself a speech therapist. I'm so relieved to finally have it done!"

"I thought you were already a speech

therapist. Isn't that your job, or am I confused?"

Ginger giggled. "Yes and no. I had the degree and one of my two internships done, but to practice independently, I had to finish this. Technically, I have the same job, but now I'll get paid more."

Marley grinned and lifted her water in a toast. "Awesome! I'm glad you're back now. It's been nice to be home, but it felt funny without you around."

Ginger rolled her eyes and brushed her hair behind her shoulders. Ginger's hair was a glossy, rich brown that swung around her shoulders when she moved. With a huff, Ginger eyed Marley. "Try being me without you here for over a decade! You're my bestie, and I only got to see you a few times a year. Go ahead and give me grief for being gone when you finally decided to move back, but you won't get any guilt out of me."

Marley shrugged. "I wasn't trying to make you feel guilty. I just missed you."

Ginger's eyes sobered. "No worries. I'm so happy you're here. Are you doing okay?" Her voice softened as she looked at Marley.

Marley had called Ginger the night of the robbery after the police left. Ginger was the friend she called when she needed to talk. With a breath, Marley met Ginger's eyes. "I'm okay, just okay. I'm more glad than I can say to finally be home. I'd rather I finally decided to come home for different reasons, but I'm so relieved to be here."

Ginger's eyes coasted over her before she nodded firmly. "Okay then. I was all worried I'd need to be ready to convince you to stay here, but I'm not getting that vibe."

Marley shook her head. "Nope. Don't get me wrong, I'm glad I spent the time I did in Seattle. I made tons of connections and learned a lot. But I'm not a city girl. I don't want to run a big tech company anymore. Trust me, I got a serious reality check on that. I just want to do some programming, keep up my work on app development and hopefully make enough with freelance work. You're stuck with me now."

Ginger's eyes flashed when she grinned, quickly sobering again. "Because you know I'm not one to avoid things, how are you sleeping? Or better yet, are you sleeping?"

Marley had talked to her several times after the robbery, so Ginger knew she'd barely slept for days afterwards. "Much better. It helped a lot just to get the hell out of my old apartment. I also did what you suggested and saw a therapist for a few weeks before I moved. The police gave me a few names. I didn't know if it would help for such a short time, but she gave me some things to do when my mind starts going in circles. Being back in Diamond Creek at the old cabin has also done wonders for my sleep."

Ginger chuckled. A waitress approached and took their order. When she left, Ginger absently twirled a lock of hair around her finger. "Okay, so we got that out of the way. What's this I hear about Last Frontier Lodge reopening? Rumor has it that's actually happening. Rumor also has it that you've been seen on the premises with the new owner who is alleged to be all kinds of sexy." Ginger tilted her head and arched a brow.

Marley fought her blush and completely failed, which led to Ginger's mouth dropping open.

"Spill it," Ginger ordered.

Marley wrestled with her thoughts for a moment and tidied the condiments. Ginger cleared her throat. Marley glanced up to find Ginger's blue eyes pinned on her, her brow arching even higher.

"Well, I can confirm the rumors. Last Frontier Lodge is reopening, and I've been on the premises. The new owner is Gage Hamilton, and he might be pretty damn sexy."

Ginger squealed. "Awesome! I can't wait for the lodge to open. Do you remember how much fun we had there when we were kids?"

Marley nodded and started to speak, but Ginger kept going. "Who is Gage Hamilton and how did you meet him? You're blushing like crazy, so you'd better fill me in on anything else."

Marley provided a quick summary on Gage's plans to reopen the lodge. When it came to filling Ginger in on exactly what transpired between her and Gage, she hesitated. She wasn't purposefully trying to hide anything, but it felt so fresh, so new, and such uncharted territory for her, she wasn't sure how to talk about it. But she desperately needed someone to talk to.

"Okay, you're getting weird. What happened?" Ginger asked.

Marley shifted in her seat and fiddled with her fork, rocking it between her fingers. Their waitress arrived with their pizza, offering a brief distraction. After a few bites, Marley looked up to find Ginger waiting expectantly. Ginger knew her so well. They'd watched each other make it through high school crushes and been each other's long-distance support for any and all relationship matters. Ginger had managed to get married and divorced already, keeping Marley busier on the side of emotional support. Marley, on the other hand, had all but ceased activity on the dating and relationship front once she finished college. She'd buckled down and worked crazy long hours. She'd never felt particularly comfortable in the dating scene, usually feeling awkward and out of place.

If anyone could give her advice, it would be Ginger. Marley took a breath and filled her in. By the time she finished, Ginger's jaw hung open. Marley crossed and uncrossed her legs and took a bite of pizza to give her something to do.

"You're telling me you had this crazy, hot night of sex and you only saw him once since then to take pictures of the lodge?"

Ginger didn't even try to keep the incredulity out of her tone.

Marley nodded, her blush returning in force. "I mean, I don't know if it was crazy…" She couldn't quite bring herself to say aloud that she was practically salivating to see him again. She'd *never* been like this about a man.

"For you, that's crazy. I'd started to wonder if you'd ever date again. The last thing I expected was for you to come home, meet a super hot guy, and go wild for a night. So what now?"

Marley brushed her hair away from her face when she leaned forward for a sip of water. "I don't know what now. I had no idea any of this was going to happen. I don't know what to think, or do. I'm supposed to go over tomorrow to review some of the stuff I've done on the website." She sighed and pushed her plate away. "This is why I didn't date for so long. I'm terrible at this. I don't know if all he wants is a one-night stand or just a short, meaningless fling, or something else. I'm all tied up and don't know how to be casual. It's awful."

Just talking about it sent her heart racing and her stomach twirling with flutters.

Gage was…everything she wasn't. She didn't doubt that he had gobs more sexual experience than she did, and with his looks, he could have his pick of women. Why he'd want to be with her, she didn't know. And she'd gone and given in the other night, potentially ruining a chance at a good friendship with him. She envisioned endless awkward moments ahead.

Ginger sighed. "Marley, snap out of it. You're getting all worked up before you know if you need to be worked up. Didn't you say he asked if you were avoiding him?"

At Marley's nod, Ginger continued. "Some guy who's only after a quick night of fun does not ask that. If that were the case, he'd be happy you were avoiding him."

"But I'm working on the website for him…"

Ginger waved at her, cutting her off. "He could easily get out of that. Stop it. You're totally cute, you always have been. You just had your brain buried in computers and books so much, you never even noticed the guys checking you out. The fact that Gage has enough sense to do something about it gives him points as far as I'm concerned. How about I come up with you tomorrow? I can meet him and let you know what I think."

"Won't that be weird to randomly bring you up there?" Marley could seriously use Ginger's opinion, but she didn't want to make Gage think she was sending scouts in to check him out.

"Hon, people are going to be randomly dropping by there every day now. I ran into Don Peters at the gas station this morning, and he was on his way to work there. That's another mark in Gage's favor if you ask me. Don said he offered him his old job back the first time he stopped by. Smart business move, but also a nice guy move. Don's all sentimental about it."

Marley's heart clenched at that small bit of news. Don had been doing okay in the years since Sandy died, but her parents had worried about him, saying he was at loose ends. If anyone loved Last Frontier Lodge, it was Don and Sandy. The only downside to Gage's kindness in offering Don his old job was it made Marley like Gage even more. Considering that she could hardly stop thinking about him, it didn't help for her to start fawning over him on another level. She was turning into a full-blown fool over him.

With a sigh, she met Ginger's eyes. "Okay then. How about you meet me at my place tomorrow morning? We can go over together. I can use all the advice I can get."

Ginger squealed while Marley shook her head. After they left the restaurant, Marley headed to one of her favorite beaches for a short walk. The tourists had mostly left town, and the beach was empty of people. Marley walked along the damp sand where the tide had rolled out. Gulls circled and called above. A pair of eagles sat side by side on a piece of driftwood, both staring out over the water. They didn't move as she approached, accustomed to people walking on the shore. They sat tall and majestic, their piercing yellow eyes tracking her as she passed in front of them. A loon floated on the water, rocking gently in the waves. The salty breeze was cold, chilling her through. With a last look at the mountains, their peaks bright white against the sky and the snow almost to the foothills now, Marley turned and walked back to her car.

When she got home, she checked her email and had a cryptic and confusing message asking her what she'd done with the data from human resources at her last job.

Marley quickly closed her laptop, unclear who sent the message since it showed up under a general mailbox address for human resources. A prickle snaked under her skin. She'd never had anything to do with data from human resources. The email had to be a mistake. Something told her not to respond, so she didn't.

CHAPTER 9

Gage stepped around a boulder on the trail as he walked alongside Don. Gage had finished painting this morning and headed up the ski trails to see how Don was faring. Don had shown up at first light with fresh coffee from Misty Mountain Café, which Gage had come to learn was a local favorite for coffee and baked goods. Gage was beyond relieved to have Don's expertise on handling the trail-side of running a ski lodge. Don had spent the morning checking the condition of the trails and ski lifts.

The air held a bite with sharp gusts of wind cutting through the trees. When they reached an area where the trails intersected, they finally paused. Gage turned and looked down the trail. The sun was high, wispy clouds moved quickly across the sky. The mountain range across the bay was taller than those surrounding Diamond Creek. Gage measured the approach of winter by the pace at which snow covered the mountains on the other side. He expected snow to fly at the lodge any day now. A pair of magpies burst out of the spruce trees, chattering loudly. They swooped to a landing on the small building beside the ski lift, winks of iridescent blue and green flashing as they settled in place.

Don walked over to the lift, checking it over. "Your best bet is going to be to replace all the lifts. Their condition is poor, seeing as they've sat through roughly twenty winters with no maintenance. As far as the trails go, I can clear the areas where debris has built up by the end of the week." He stepped to Gage's side and leaned against the building. "I see you've already taken care of the paint on all of these."

Gage nodded. "Yup. I'm trying to get the exterior work done by next week. Aside from paint and some roof repairs, things were okay. There are a few aesthetics I could address, but I'll probably wait until next summer for that." He considered what Don had said. He knew he needed to sink some money into the lodge. He hoped he had enough with what Gram had left him and his own savings though he wasn't particularly worried. His years as a SEAL involved all work and no play. Without a family to support, he'd socked away any extra money into his savings, so he had a cushion.

Don nodded approvingly. "You've done a lot. If you keep it up, you'll have the paint done by next week. As for the lifts..."

"Let's replace them. Any suggestions on where we'd go to take care of that?"

Don chuckled. "We'll use the same place your grandparents used to order that type of equipment. If you'll let me, I'll take a look at your Gram's old files. I handled all that stuff back in the day. Happy to do it now."

Gage experienced a wave of relief, followed immediately with a mix of euphoria and anxiety. He'd dreamed of being back in Diamond Creek since the day they moved away. Visits during his childhood had only stoked his dreams. He hadn't realized it, but somewhere along the way, after he went from boy to man and faced the devastating realities of war and paid the price of grief, he'd lost hope of ever returning to Diamond Creek. When Gram had died, he'd thought he had to do what adults did and absorb another loss in his heart. He missed her terribly because she'd been the kind of grandmother any child would be lucky to have—a warm, kind, ever-supportive cheerleader who offered blunt advice usually when it was most needed. The surprise inheritance of Last Frontier Lodge, which he'd thought long ago sold, had opened up the portal to his forgotten dream. Don's entrance into his world here made the logistical realities of his dream seem possible. Yet, Gage couldn't quite believe it would all be possible.

Without a word, Don pushed away from the building and began to walk back down the trail. He glanced over his shoulder. "Let's head back down, so I can take a look at the old orders. I'd like to have those lifts on the way as soon as we can."

Gage began walking down the trail behind Don. He enjoyed what little time he'd had to work with Don. Don was comfortable with quiet and tended to only speak when necessary. He worked steadily and with clear focus. His style meshed well with Gage's. As they moved down the trail, Gage thought of Marley. He'd resisted the urge to ask Don more questions about her. He was more than a little curious to know more about her, and it was clear Don knew her and her family well. He also couldn't think of her without considering the robbery Don had told him about. He sensed Don had told him all he knew about that, so he avoided further questions. He'd reached out to a former SEAL team member, Aidan McNamara, who worked in private security in Seattle now. Gage hoped Aidan could use his contacts with the local police to ascertain the status of Marley's robbery and assault. With Marley moving out of state, Gage knew the pressure on the authorities to investigate would ease. Aidan had assured him he'd look into it and get back to him.

In the meantime, Gage was battling the fury he felt every moment he considered it. This feeling rode alongside his confusion about how Marley had shimmied her way past his defenses without the slightest effort. Her utter lack of artifice drew him like a moth to a flame. He couldn't conceive of trying to put some distance between them, but it went against all of his well-established boundaries around relationships, namely that he didn't have them. When she'd called to say she'd be out of town for two days, he'd been startled at the lurch in his heart. Unbeknownst to him on a conscious level, he'd been counting on seeing her. Since she returned, she'd stopped by briefly to take some pictures of the lodge for the website. Her brief visit had stoked his wish to see her more. Though he wouldn't deny she drew him like a magnet physically, it was more than that. He craved simply being near her and was bound and determined he'd see her tonight.

Don turned the corner around the side of the lodge to head for the front entrance when Gage heard him exclaim. "Marley girl!" Don's hearty greeting was followed by the softer sound of Marley's voice and another female voice. All he was focused on was the knowledge that Marley was here. His heart thumped—hard—and his body tightened.

He jogged around the building to find Marley wrapped in a bear hug from Don.

When Don set her down, Marley's eyes met his. Gage felt the instant pull of his attraction to her. Her auburn hair was tousled from the wind, her cheeks bright. He reined in the urge to walk to her and kiss her plump mouth. With the knowledge of the most amazing night he'd ever experienced and what Don had told him, he couldn't think clearly. She smiled in his direction and gestured to the woman with her whom he hadn't even bothered to glance at yet.

"Gage, this is Ginger. We grew up in Diamond Creek together. She heard you were opening the lodge again and wanted to stop by."

Gage nodded and forced his eyes away from Marley. Ginger was gorgeous with shiny brown hair that swung around her shoulders, wide blue eyes, and a broad smile. Gage had absolutely zero interest in her and had to work to keep his gaze from traveling back to Marley. She was like a magnet. He drew upon his ingrained manners and smiled politely. "Nice to meet you."

Ginger's smile widened. "When I heard you were opening the lodge again, I didn't believe it, but Marley says it's true. I'm so excited! You have no idea how happy this is going to make the town. We've all missed the lodge." Ginger bounced on her feet.

"I'm definitely getting the idea that it's news for me to re-open the lodge. With Marley's help on the website and Don's help around here, I'm hoping I can pull it off." Gage was conflicted at the excitement around town about the lodge. On the one hand, it fed his efforts. On the other, he worried he couldn't meet the high expectations.

"You'd better have it ready before Christmas because you've already got a few online reservations," Marley said with a grin.

Gage swung his gaze back to her. "Seriously?"

Marley nodded, her mossy green eyes sparkling. Gage had to tamp down the urge to swing her into his arms. Don chuckled. "Told you hiring her was a smart move. But we've got work to do. Show me where the files are and I'll get those lifts ordered." Don paused and glanced between Marley and Ginger. "You two know anyone who might want a job handling the reception and housekeeping end of things here? Gage is about ten steps ahead of himself in his brain, and we need some staff lined up yesterday."

Marley shrugged. "I can ask my mom, but I'm not much help in that area since I just moved back. Any ideas, Ginger?"

Ginger tapped her finger on her cheek. "Let me think. I know I can come up with some ideas. You need to put some ads in the classified section online for the local paper." She addressed her last comment to Marley. Gage almost laughed aloud at how quickly Ginger had ascertained he'd be useless in that area.

Marley's eyes widened as she looked from Ginger to Gage. "I don't know..."

Ginger put her hands on her hips. "If you're in charge of the online stuff, this is your thing."

Gage couldn't hold back his grin when Marley flushed and nodded. He didn't plan it this way, but every tiny way she was involved with the lodge notched joy in his heart.

Don chuckled and turned to walk into the lodge. "Let's get inside. It's freezing. You girls can boss Gage around while I go through my old files."

A while later, Ginger had left to bring

takeout pizza back to the lodge. Once Don located the old records of the companies he used for ordering the lodge equipment, Marley had looked online and set him up to search for what he needed. Gage had busied himself with a few lingering repairs in some of the rooms.

It was hard to be in the room with Marley and keep his hands off of her. He was meandering in uncharted territory with her and the other night was fresh in his mind and body. He didn't know how she'd have felt if he did what he wanted to do in front of Don and Ginger, nor did he trust himself to manage the wildfire that simmered between them. So he kept busy and left her to help Don.

He finished adding oil to the hinges on all the doors in one of the wings of the lodge when he heard his name. He stepped out from behind the door. "Right here."

"Oh, there you are. We have pizza," Ginger said, beckoning for him to follow.

He grabbed his toolbox, quickly tucking everything away, and began to follow her. Ginger paused in the hall to wait for him. When he reached her side, her eyes coasted over him, her gaze assessing.

"Did I mention I'm happy you're opening the lodge again?"

Gage nodded. "You did." He sensed she wanted to say something else, but he wasn't going to prod.

She took a breath. "I just met you, and my gut tells me you're a good guy. I have to say this because Marley's my best friend, so if you take offense, you'll have to get over it. I'm not sure what your intentions are with Marley, but whatever you do, you'd better be good to her. She's been through a lot lately. I don't want to see her get hurt."

Gage's heart tightened. It occurred to him that no one had ever warned him in this way about a woman. He'd gone through most of his adult life focused on his career in the military. It hadn't been by design, but he'd kept relationships casual. After Matt died and he came home, he hadn't considered himself decent company and was battling enough of his own demons that he didn't want to foist them on anyone else. But Marley was something he hadn't seen coming. He wanted to assure Ginger she didn't need to worry, but he didn't even know what his intentions were. He did know he'd do anything in his power to keep her from being hurt. The bare facts Don had reported to him about the night Marley was robbed flashed through his mind.

He met Ginger's eyes. "I don't know what to say other than that I have no intention of hurting Marley. I'm not sure what she told you…"

Ginger cut him off. "More than enough. Maybe I shouldn't say this, but I will. Marley doesn't exactly have much experience with men. If you haven't noticed, she likes to keep her brain busy. Don't go thinking she gossiped about you two, but I've known her long enough, I know when something's up. I forced it out of her."

Gage nodded. "It's okay. To be honest, I'm glad you said something. Marley's…special. I'm not sure where things are going with us." He paused, holding back the questions bubbling up inside. Ginger waited patiently. Gage realized perhaps she could help him. He wanted to know Marley better. He also wanted to know what Ginger knew about the robbery. He was determined to track down who was behind it. Any information Ginger offered, he could pass on to Aidan.

"Don told me about the robbery. Marley

hasn't mentioned it, and I don't want to make her uncomfortable, but anything you can tell me would be good. I've got a friend in Seattle who's in touch with the police there. I don't want the investigation to wither just because she's not around pressuring them. If she's talked to you about it, maybe we have some more info to pass on."

Ginger's eyes widened. She studied him for a long moment before nodding slowly. "I'll be happy to tell you everything she told me, but not now. For what it's worth, maybe you don't know where things are going with you and Marley, but you might want to face the reality that she obviously means something to you. You wouldn't be so concerned about her if she didn't."

Gage nodded tightly. Ginger's observation wasn't news to him, but damn if he knew what to do with it. He was used to being in control. Marley was entirely out of his scope of planning, and he felt helpless to control his feelings about her. He shifted on his feet and rolled his shoulders. "Not denying it, but that's about all I have to add on that. How about I set up a call with my friend in the next few days? I can conference you in. He's already gotten the entire police file on it." He held Ginger's gaze for another moment. "I'm not letting whoever did that to Marley walk away. As for your warning, no worries. It's good to know Marley has a friend like you."

Ginger grinned and began walking again. "Let's go eat."

CHAPTER 10

*M*arley flicked on the lights downstairs in her cabin and quickly put some logs in the woodstove for a fire. November was racing by with Thanksgiving right around the corner. Winter was nipping on the heels of autumn. Ginger had driven away a few minutes ago. Their impromptu pizza dinner with Gage and Don had been more than nice. The simple joy of being home and having dinner with friends was enough to make her day. Adding Gage to the mix only made it better. Though it had been challenging to be near him and keep her hands to herself. All he had to do was exist in space near her and attraction buzzed to life, its current snapping between them.

Ginger had given him her enthusiastic stamp of approval. On the short drive back to Marley's cabin where Ginger had left her car, Ginger demanded that Marley promise she wouldn't get in her own way with Gage. Though Marley didn't disagree with Ginger, she wasn't as certain of what Gage may want. Ginger had been adamant that her gut told her good things about Gage, and it was worth it for Marley to throw caution to the wind. Marley only wished she could take that advice and act on it so easily. The depth of her attraction to Gage and the feelings bubbling to life frightened her. It was beyond anything she'd experienced or expected, and she didn't want to let herself hope for something that couldn't be.

She forced her mind off of Gage and to the moment, tucking a few pieces of tinder under the logs and lighting the fire. Once the flames caught, she closed the glass door to the woodstove. She grabbed her laptop off the desk in the corner and sat down on the couch to work on a few things. While she was fiddling with the placement of photos of the lodge website, her email pinged. By habit, she clicked on it to check. Another email from the same general human resources address sat in her inbox. This email again had no name, although it was more specific than the first one, specifically asking if she had retained possession of a flash drive with human resources data on it and warning her she was obligated to return all company property.

Her fingers sat on her keyboard. She began to type a reply, but again hesitated. Fear flickered inside. She didn't know why, but this didn't feel right. She'd never been involved with human resources data at her former job. Her extent of involvement with human resources had revolved solely around her own hiring and resignation. She'd been pleasantly surprised at how friendly her main contact there had been. Something told her that whoever was emailing her likely didn't even work in the human resources department. She resisted going there, but her mind kept circling over the night of her robbery and the way the man had torn through her apartment. He'd said little and she'd been so stunned, terrified and hurt. After he'd whipped her across the face with his gun, he'd shoved her in the corner where she'd remained and watched him. She'd noticed that he seemed focused on her computer area, dumping out drawers, stealing all of her flash drives and equipment. He'd also stolen her television and other electronics, but it had appeared to be an afterthought. She didn't want to think it, but she was afraid these emails had something to do with that night.

A knock at the door startled her, her heart jumpstarting as fear clogged in her throat. She suddenly couldn't recall if she'd locked her door. Her eyes swung wildly to the door, a tiny wave of relief rising when she saw the bolt was turned. She looked around and realized there was nowhere to hide here. The cabin windows offered a full view of the living room. She couldn't think of who would come by at this hour. Her parents were nearby, but they would have called. If Ginger had forgotten something, she would have called as well.

There was another knock at the door and a muffled voice. Marley finally uncurled her legs and set her laptop on the table beside the couch. She forced herself to stand and walk to the door, her heart battering against her ribcage.

"Yes?"

"Marley, it's Gage."

She closed her eyes and fought back tears. The relief was so intense, she needed a moment to pull herself together. She didn't know why he was here, but she knew he was safe. After a few deep breaths, she turned the bolt and opened the door.

Gage leaned against the doorframe, one arm hooked above his head, his gray eyes locking with hers immediately. There he stood, his jacket hanging open, his sculpted chest outlined by his fitted t-shirt, and jeans resting low on his hips. Her pulse quickened and heat twisted inside. "Hey, I..." He paused, his eyes coasting over her face. "Are you okay?"

She opened her mouth to reply, but no words came. The panicky feeling inside was receding, but her chest was tight and her breathing shallow. The combined feelings of frantic fear from the moments before she knew it was Gage and the spark of attraction between them short-circuited her brain. She gulped in air and tried to bring her body under control. Gage's eyes sharpened. A sharp gust of cold air blew through the door.

He moved quickly and stepped inside, pulling the door shut behind him. The icy air swirled around them. She couldn't seem to move and simply stood there and stared at him. His eyes shifted from questioning to concerned. "Marley, talk to me. You look scared. What's going on?"

She took a breath, this time managing to breathe more slowly. She took a step away from the door. "I, uh..." She felt tears welling and fought them back. *You cannot fall apart in front of Gage. Pull it together.* Her stern internal dialogue was no match for her body's instinctive fear reflex, which had kicked into gear the moment an unexpected knock came at the door. Hugging her arms around her waist, she took another few steps back and bumped against the kitchen counter.

Gage remained where he stood by the door, appearing to sense she needed the space. His eyes were locked to hers. Unable to bear it, she closed her eyes, a tear splashing on her cheek as she did. She held still and forced herself to breathe in and out slowly, reminding herself over and over that she was in Diamond Creek, safe in her cabin with Gage nearby—nowhere near her old apartment in Seattle. Her heartbeat slowed, and she gained control of her breathing again. As reality sank into her consciousness, a wave of mortification washed through her. Gage would think she was crazy. She had no idea how to explain her reaction to a simple knock on her door. Though she wished she could keep her eyes closed, only opening them after he dissolved into thin air, she knew she had no choice but to face him. So, she opened her eyes. To find him leaning against a stool by the counter, his elbow hooked over it. His eyes were on her. He looked coiled tight, as if he was holding back.

But when he met her eyes, his gray gaze softened. The room was quiet. Uncertain what to say, she watched him. He started to speak and then stopped. He traced the edge of the counter with his fingertip. Her eyes followed the motion.

"I'm not sure if I should say this, but Don told me what happened in Seattle."

His simple sentence slammed into her. For a moment, she was annoyed Don had told him. But then she was relieved. At some point, he'd have heard from someone. It might as well be sooner, rather than later.

And from someone who cared, not from someone being gossipy. His finger traveled back and forth along the corner of the counter. She slowly lifted her eyes to his and nodded. "I'm glad he got that out of the way for me." She gestured in the direction of the door. "When you knocked, I didn't know it was you. I'm sorry, I didn't mean to freak out."

He shook his head sharply. "Don't apologize. I should have called. It's completely reasonable you'd get scared if someone shows up unannounced."

She nodded slowly and shrugged. "I guess so. I just didn't want you to think it had anything to do with you." She paused and glanced to the fire in the woodstove. The room looked so warm, cozy and homey. It was hard to believe she could ever be frightened here, but she had been. "Do you want to sit down?" she finally asked.

He glanced to her, to the woodstove and back again. "I don't have to stay."

Fierce longing raced through her. She didn't want him to leave. At all. His quiet strength was a balm to her shattered nerves, the soft current between them almost a comfort though it tied her up inside if she tried to think about what it meant. "Please stay. I mean, unless you…"

"I'll stay," he said with alacrity. He pushed away from the stool and followed her to the couch.

When they sat down, her eyes automatically traveled to her laptop, wondering again who was behind the emails. Gage was more in tune than she'd have liked him to be. He instantly followed her gaze, his eyes meeting hers. He arched a brow. It both comforted her and confused her that he picked up on her feelings.

"What?" she asked.

"What was that look for?" he countered.

Marley considered whether to tell him and figured she might as well. He might think she was crazy, but there was no sense in hiding it. She quickly explained.

He studied her for a long moment before speaking. "I don't like it. It doesn't make sense."

"It's weird. I can't tell if I'm freaking out over nothing after what happened in Seattle, or if I should be worried." What she didn't say was his mere presence soothed her. When he was near, she felt safe and secure. That itself rattled her a little, but she didn't feel like questioning it now.

"Would you mind if I asked a friend to trace the emails?"

"You could do that?"

"Well, not me specifically. I have a friend who works in private security. This kind of thing is right up his alley. Or maybe you could on your own. Computers are your thing after all."

Marley rolled her eyes. "I do coding and development. I'm not a hacker. Maybe I'd have a leg up on some people if I wanted to figure it out, but it's not the kind of thing I've spent much time on. If you have a friend who'd be willing to check it out, that'd be great. Even if we find out I'm just being silly, that's better than what I'm doing right now."

"You got it. I'll call him tomorrow and see what he needs from us to make it happen."

Marley leaned back into the couch, tension starting to ease from her body. She glanced over at Gage. His eyes were intent on her. "You okay now?"

"Yeah. I'm going to have to get used to the fact that sometimes people will knock on the door unexpectedly and learn how to deal with it."

The embers of heat that Gage elicited sparked to life when she looked back at him. The couch was tiny, so even though he was in the opposite corner he was right beside her. He moved swiftly, wrapping his arm around her and tugging her onto his lap. His body was all hard muscles and heat. The desire buzzing between them snapped and crackled. He met her eyes, his smoky gaze mesmerizing her.

"I don't like seeing you scared like that. No matter what, we're going to make sure they find whoever hurt you." His words fell fiercely into the quiet, his voice rough and raw.

Unable to speak over the thundering of her pulse, she simply nodded. In a flash, his lips were on hers, his kiss hot, wet, and devouring. The twisting heat inside of her tightened and unfurled, spinning through her veins. She couldn't get close enough. His touch was everywhere. She tumbled into the moment, losing all sense of time. Clothes were torn off. His hard muscles rippled under her hands as she explored him. His lips and hands traced her body. The roughened skin of his palms was flint to her desire. Hot, achy, and burning for him, she scrambled up and pushed him back on the couch. Straddling his legs, she pushed her tangled hair away from her face.

Gage reached up and stroked a hand through her hair, his palm cupping her cheek and sliding down the side of her neck, coming to rest between her breasts. She couldn't recall how it had come to be, but they were both bare. Hot, liquid need pulsed through her. He suddenly lifted her, turning her until she rested before him on the couch. His smoky eyes locked with hers. Her breath was shallow, her pulse racing. He slowly slid his palms up her calves, pushing her knees apart as he did. His hands traveled up her thighs, pausing at the juncture where she pulsed with need. He leaned forward and brought his mouth to her.

Her vision blurred as she fell into the rush of sensation. He took his time, his fingers plunging in and out of her while he dragged his tongue through her folds and over her clit—over and over until she was incoherent with need. Her hips were restless, but he held her firm with one strong hand gripping her in place. He wound her tighter and tighter until he finally drew her clit in his mouth, the sharp spike of sensation pushing her over the edge. Her climax wracked her and left her shaking as he slowly pulled away.

"Marley..."

His rough voice elicited a shiver, need arcing again in the aftermath. That's what he did to her...with nothing more than the sound of his voice. She dragged her eyes open to find his waiting. He was on his knees in front of her, his body taut. He lifted a hand and stroked it up her abdomen, the backs of his fingers barely dusting her skin, his touch unbearably arousing. Longing clenched her in its grip.

He shifted and snagged his jeans off the floor, pulling a condom out of the pocket. He tore it open with his teeth and swiftly rolled it on, eyes on hers the whole time. Vibrating with need, she waited as he shifted his weight forward, his cock, hard and hot, coming to rest between her folds. She began to chase ecstasy again, following him into the storm.

Her breath came in ragged gasps when he proceeded to drive her wild by slowly dragging the head of his cock back and forth in her slick folds. When his name fell from her lips in a gasp, he finally gave her what she needed and lifted her hips as he slowly surged into her channel. The relief was so acute, she almost came instantly, but he held himself still. Closing her eyes, she savored the sensation of fullness, arching her back and pushing her hips against him until he was fully seated within her. Her channel throbbed around him.

"Look at me," he whispered.

By force of will, she managed to open her eyes and meet his. Only then did he begin to move, rolling his hips against her while she began to move in rhythm with him. The moment between them lengthened into a blur, hot and electric. Sensation teemed within her. She lost herself in the push and pull of him inside of her, each surge driving her higher. Slow, long, hot, and deep strokes pushed her closer and closer. Pleasure built in waves until she thundered to the edge and toppled over with a cry, flying apart in his arms. With a muffled shout, he arched into her, shuddering against her. He held still over her before slowly shifting down, immediately locking his arms around her and rolling them, so he was under her. Her head tucked into the crook of his neck, she slowly settled, her orgasm echoing through her body.

Marley only wanted to stay there forever, locked in the protective cradle of his embrace, his heartbeat thudding against hers, his hand softly stroking her hair. After an indeterminate amount of time, it could have been as little as a few minutes or as long as an hour, Gage spoke. "You're getting cold. Let's get upstairs."

When his hand stroked down her back, she felt the goose bumps rise under his palm.

"Oh." She slowly lifted her head and sat up. When she glanced down at him, her heart clenched. His smoky gray eyes were there, waiting for hers. The corner of his mouth hooked up. The firelight flickered over his skin and want arced through her again. That's what he did to her. She met his gaze and smiled ruefully. "I suppose I should get up."

He shrugged. "Fine with me if you stay right there, but we might be more comfortable in your bed."

* * *

GAGE CARRIED MARLEY UPSTAIRS, thinking he could hold her all day and it would never get old. Her body was soft and lush. He glanced down and caught sight of the freckles scattered across her cheeks. He'd discovered she had smatters of freckles all over her body, which he loved. They were her constellations, and he'd suddenly become enamored with astronomy. She giggled when he set her on the bed.

"I can walk, you know."

"I know, but I like to carry you."

He quickly stepped into the bathroom adjacent to her bedroom and disposed of his condom. When he returned to the bedroom, he lifted the quilt and wrapped it around them tightly. She shivered, her skin pebbling against his. He'd never understood the desire to snuggle, but with Marley, it was sheer heaven. She draped herself against him, her foot stroking down his calf as she tucked her leg over his. He tugged her close and breathed deep, listening to her breathing slow and become even.

He was half out of his mind over her and didn't know what the hell he was going to do about it. But he couldn't conceive of stopping whatever was happening between them. His mind flicked back to the fear he saw in her eyes when she answered the door. Cold anger flashed through him. He would find whoever put that fear in her eyes.

CHAPTER 11

"Any update from the police?" Gage asked, the phone tucked against his shoulder as he tossed papers into the shredder. He was ruthlessly going through the old business files. After noting any pertinent information, he was shredding almost everything. He'd decided to call Aidan and try to get some movement on the police investigation of Marley's robbery.

"Not much. All they have is what they have. As far as robberies and assaults go, it's not much. The guy wore a mask and gloves, so we have no fingerprints and no easy way to ID the guy from the surveillance cameras at the building. Marley gave them a good list of what was stolen, but even if something turns up, usually it will have been pawned and resold," Aidan replied.

"Fuck. That's not good enough. I'm going to talk with her friend here and see if she has anything to add. She called her friend the night of the robbery. Maybe she missed a detail with the police. I also want you to follow up on an email she got…" He quickly filled Aidan in on his concerns about the email.

There was a long silence after he spoke. "Aidan? You still there?"

Aidan chuckled. "I'm here. Just wondering exactly who this Marley is. She seems, uh, pretty important to you."

Gage experienced a flash of anger. His need to protect Marley was fierce. "So what?"

"So, I don't know if you ever got involved with any women for more than a few dates, if that. I don't mean you're a player, more that you don't play. At all. If you like Marley, it's a good thing if you ask me."

"I didn't ask you." His anger flared again. He didn't particularly care to field questions about Marley. He was struggling enough to adjust to how she made him feel.

Aidan's laugh was full this time. "No, you

didn't. But you're a good guy, and I think it might do you good to care about someone."

Aidan's comment hit home, piercing right to the heart of why Gage kept women at a distance. Aidan had been on his Navy SEAL team with Matt. He knew how close they were. Matt had been one of Aidan's best friends too. But Aidan hadn't watched from a distance when the helicopter carrying Matt exploded in the air, knowing that his body would fall in pieces along with the helicopter and its other occupants and there wasn't a damn thing he could do but watch helplessly. Gage preferred to feel in control and as if he had the possibility to do something. Matt's death had been a bleak reminder of the fact that life always threw curve balls. The only thing he had control of in that situation was how he managed his feelings. The possibility of doing something to change the outcome didn't exist. Gage breathed deeply, forcing the painful memory out of his mind. Aidan was a good friend and meant the best.

"Maybe so," Gage finally replied. He took another breath, his next comment startling him as much as it likely did Aidan. "Marley's something else. I think you'd like her."

"I'm sure I would. I'd love to meet her sometime. Meanwhile, I'll look into that email thing as soon as I can and let you know what I find. I'll also keep prodding the police."

Gage tossed his phone on the desk and walked to the window. The office window faced the slopes. Don was up there working. Gage had quickly realized that Don's willingness to return to his old job was going to be a major reason he managed to open the lodge. Gage wouldn't have known where to start when it came to running the lifts. He probably could have fumbled his way through, but it would have been by the seat of his pants. For Don though, it was old hat. Gage also appreciated the fact that Don clearly savored the work. He was busy from sunup until sundown every day, checking in with Gage as he went along. He'd promised his daughter would stop by today to talk about running the kitchen.

Marley meandered into Gage's thoughts —her flashing green eyes and those tiny freckles dotting her skin. She stood in the wings of his thoughts all the time now. His feelings for her had created a situation he'd never encountered. Aidan's point was accurate. Gage didn't get emotionally involved with women. Distance worked just fine for him. It was clean and uncomplicated, and he could maintain control that way. But he'd never been tempted. He'd thought for years it was a choice, yet now that Marley had blown his well-honed defenses to bits without lifting a finger, he wondered if his control had been an illusion. He simply hadn't met the woman who mattered enough to tempt him. With Marley, he had. He rolled his shoulders, uncomfortable with the depth of his feelings. He didn't want to push her away. Frankly, he couldn't conceive of that. He couldn't say precisely why, but she tugged at him—down deep. Aside from the fact that his attraction to her was flat off the charts, he liked her. She was practical, smart, funny and loyal. If he'd been asked to say what mattered to him in a person, Marley was all of those things and more—the ephemeral electricity that sparked between them was undeniable.

The look in her eyes when she opened the door last night tightened his chest. If he thought much about what had happened, he wasn't sure what he might do. For now, he'd make sure she was safe and coordinate with

Aidan to look into things in Seattle. When he'd woken beside her this morning, her auburn hair bright against the pillow, her legs loosely tangled with his, it occurred to him that he assumed he'd be with her every night. He wasn't so sure he was ready for that, nor her. But he wanted her to be safe, and he knew she'd be safe if she were with him. Besides, it just felt...right.

He sighed and ran a hand through his hair. Glancing around the office, he noted that he was almost done with the files. He tugged the last file drawer open and plowed through it. After he was done, he texted Marley to tell her he'd be by later. When he walked out of the office, he heard voices toward the front. He made his way out there and found Don leaning against the reception desk talking with an unfamiliar woman.

As soon as the woman turned toward him, he knew she had to be Don's daughter. She had Don's blue eyes and smile paired with honey gold hair.

"You must be Delia," Gage said as he approached them.

Don chuckled and winked. "That she is." He turned to Delia." Honey, this is Gage. His grandparents used to run this place and he's taking over. He's desperate for a cook."

Delia's smile was wide as she strode to Gage, her hand held out. Her grip was strong and firm.

"It's like your dad said, I'm desperate for a cook. More specifically, I'm desperate for someone to manage the kitchen and perhaps help me hire some staff for the front here. Your dad said you might be willing to help out. I'll pay you well if you're interested."

Delia angled her head to the side. "Don't you want to interview me first?"

Gage shrugged. "I trust your dad. I don't think he'd suggest you if he didn't think it would work."

Don chuckled again, shaking his head.

Delia glanced between them. "Well, how about we play it by ear? I was with my mom all the time here. I'm not worried about the cooking part, but I can't say I've run an entire kitchen before, so we'll have to see how it goes." Her eyes became hesitant. "Are you going to mind if I bring my son with me sometimes?"

"Of course not. That's how it was with your mom. She never minded kids around. I wouldn't want it to be any different now." Gage couldn't help but smile. His memories here, those memories he'd clung to for so many years before he discarded them, were of a place he always felt welcome. He wouldn't want it any other way.

Delia's return smile was bright. "I think we have a deal. Dad tells me we have a lot to do in the next month to have this place ready to go by Christmas. When do you want me to start?"

"Tomorrow?"

Delia's eyes widened. "Tomorrow?"

Don clapped Gage on the shoulder. "Hon, I told you Gage would put you to work right away."

Delia nodded slowly. "Okay. I can probably make that work."

After a few more minutes discussing some plans, Delia went her way. Don beamed at Gage, his eyes damp. "Thank you," he said gruffly.

Gage shrugged. "I think I'm supposed to be thanking you for finding me a cook I can trust right off the bat."

Don shook his head. "It feels good to have this place on its way back. I've missed Sandy so much it hurts these last few years, but being here is nothing but good memories. It'll be pretty nice to have Delia around. Delia's been at loose ends. Went to college, fell in love, got pregnant and then got dumped. She's a damn good mom, but it hasn't been easy on her own. She was all worried about what to do about her little boy Nicholas, so you made her day by saying it'd be okay if he was here sometimes. She won't bring him everyday, but here and there it'll be nice for her. She's been working odd jobs, but hasn't found anything that works out great for her. I think this might be a good thing. That's why I'm thanking you."

Gage's chest tightened. All the years of childhood dreams of being back at the ski lodge had been so vague. He'd never considered how much this place meant to some of the people who worked here, or to the locals in Diamond Creek. As a man who'd led a private, structured life and learned the painful lessons grief had to offer, he'd responded by compartmentalizing his life, rarely allowing anyone new into his personal circle. Marley had slipped through the cracks of his heart in her own way. Don and now Delia touched another corner of his heart. He knew he was lucky to have her and Don and was happy to give her the chance to work at the lodge.

He took a breath, met Don's eyes and nodded. "Well, I guess we're even then. I'm glad it feels good on your end, but I can't tell you how glad I am you offered to come back. I don't know if I could pull this off without your help. Before I got here, I had high hopes, but I hadn't really thought through the logistics of it. Pretty damn sure I might have crashed and burned if you hadn't come along."

Don held his gaze and nodded slowly. "Glad to be here." He looked out the window. The sun was already sliding down behind the mountains even though it was only four in the afternoon. The days were shortening rapidly with winter solstice roughly a month away. Don looked back toward him. "I've gotta head back up to grab my tools before it gets dark. I'll catch you in the morning, okay?"

After Don left, Gage returned to the office and tidied the mess he'd created. He sat at his desk and quickly checked his email. Out of curiosity, he took a look at the lodge website. Marley had done a beautiful job.

Gage couldn't quite believe it, but seeing the website made his dream feel real. He clicked on the blog page and his heart clenched. Marley had taken photos of his different projects with cute captions. She'd thrown in some wildlife photos—a moose nibbling on alder by the lodge, a raven flying across one of the trails, and an eagle sitting on the sign-post. Her updates were light, breezy and inviting. He noticed she'd posted an update this morning announcing they were already almost fully booked for the week after Christmas. His heart squeezed, and he lost his breath for a moment.

His discarded childhood dream was coming true. Marley's involvement only made it sweeter, and he didn't quite know what to do with the feeling. He took another slow breath. His phone beeped, indicating a text had arrived. He glanced down to see Marley had replied to his earlier text.

Okay. What time?

His heart clenched, this time for a different reason. He hated that it was important for her to know what time, so she wouldn't be startled by his arrival. It seemed trivial, but it wasn't. After what had happened, the last thing she needed was anyone showing up unannounced. He was frustrated with himself for not thinking about that last night when he went over there. The anger he'd been trying to keep at bay flashed through him. He needed answers and fast on who was sending her those damn emails and who was behind the robbery. He knew he couldn't erase what happened for her, but he wanted her to have closure. That meant finding answers.

He glanced at his phone and typed his reply.

How about six? Can I take you out to dinner?

After long moments of staring at his phone with no reply from her yet, Gage stood and went to grab the tools he'd left in another wing. He'd methodically made his way through the lodge handling the minor interior repairs. All that was left was for him to hire a cleaning crew and then deal with the new furniture. It had already arrived, and he'd stored it in the basement until the place was cleaned.

When he returned to his office, his phone lit up with her reply.

Six works. I'm meeting Ginger at Sally's.

How about I meet you there? You're welcome to join us.

He grinned. Any chance to see Marley made him feel like a teenage boy again. Tech savvy though she was, Marley didn't engage in the banter so many others did with texting. She was short and to the point. He liked it because it was like her—without artifice. If dinner with Marley meant Ginger would be there, Gage would go along though he selfishly wanted her for himself.

MARLEY TOOK a look around Sally's as she walked in. It was just as she recalled. Sally's was a hopping local hangout—a restaurant that served basic pub fare and a bar that kept busy year round with music acts booked through every season. It was in a renovated barn with the place divided into the bar and restaurant sections. The old hayloft held overflow seating for the restaurant. She scanned the restaurant and spied Ginger sitting at a booth. She quickly made her way over and slid into the booth.

Ginger looked up from the menu and squealed. "Marley girl!"

Marley rolled her eyes and grinned. "How's it going?"

Ginger shrugged. "Nothing new except I'm gonna be giddy for months that you're finally home for good. You'll just have to put up with it."

Marley's chest tightened. It felt so good to be home, she couldn't quite believe it. "It's not hard to put up with. Safe to say, I'm just as happy as you are," she said with a grin.

A waitress arrived and took their drink order. Ginger brushed her dark hair away from her face and tucked it behind her ears. "So, what's new with Gage?"

Marley felt the flush on her face. Ginger's eyes widened. "Well then. No details needed. If you're blushing like that, then I know how last night went."

"Oh my God! How do you know something happened last night?"

"Because I left with you. So, something happened between then and now or you wouldn't be blushing."

Marley considered last night—another night when she lost herself in the wild heat that engulfed her whenever she was with Gage. She almost couldn't believe she was the same woman who'd fallen apart in his arms last night. Heat streaked through her. She shifted uncomfortably. Amazing as it was, her complete lack of control with Gage chafed at her. She was trying to get her life back under control, not lose herself in a man. The second her mind questioned it, her body remembered the feel of his rough hands on her, and she felt a ping of longing in her center.

Marley distracted herself by grabbing the menu and flipping through it. "Last night was great," she mumbled. "He's also meeting us here."

Ginger squealed again. People at nearby tables turned in their direction. "Ginger," Marley hissed. "Do you mind? It's enough that I'm talking to you about him, you don't need to make a scene. He'll be here any minute, so how about not embarrassing the hell out of me?"

Ginger sat back with a humph. "Okay, okay. I'm excited for you. You deserve something good, and he's good," she said, dragging the last word out.

Marley fought her blush and gave up with a giggle. "He's definitely good." Which was part of her problem. Gage was so good, he was knocking past her guard and she didn't know what to do about it. He was so out of the stratosphere when it came to sexy, he blew her mind with just a touch.

Ginger's eyes sobered, and she reached over to squeeze Marley's hand. "I can't help but tease, and I'm happy for you."

"Don't get too excited. I'm not really sure where things are going."

Ginger released her hand and leaned back when the waitress arrived with water and a bottle of the house red wine. Ginger waved the waitress off when she started to pour, deftly taking the bottle from her and filling both of their glasses. After a quick toast, Ginger angled her head to the side, eying Marley thoughtfully.

"What?" Marley asked.

"Just thinking maybe you should give yourself a chance to think something good might come of this thing with Gage."

Hope flashed in Marley's heart. She hadn't planned on any of this, but it was impossible for her not to want more with Gage. She immediately tried to quell the feeling. The last thing she needed to do was pin her hopes on something that couldn't go anywhere.

"I didn't say it wouldn't, just that I'm not sure where things are going."

"I know, but that's an easy way to keep him at a distance. I think he really likes you."

Marley flushed because it was hard to comprehend a man like Gage would really like her. He was the kind of man many a woman would fantasize about—a body honed to perfection, the military sexy vibe he gave off, and so good in bed, he nearly set her on fire. She'd never been known to turn heads and definitely lacked experience. When she was skin to skin with Gage, her doubts didn't crowd her mind, but outside those moments, she wasn't quite sure what to think. She had no idea what he considered them to be. It was obvious he had eons more experience than her, so for all she knew, he figured they were having a good time and when it was over, it would be over. She didn't know if she wanted it to be something else, but she wanted to feel more in control.

Ginger's voice broke into her thoughts. "I know I can't talk you into it, but you've spent most of your adult life oblivious to the guys checking you out. You were too damn busy with your work to pay attention. How about you practice making your brain shut up and just go with it?"

Marley took a sip of wine and leaned back, working to keep her expression calm. Trying to "just go with it" with Gage scared the hell out of her. He pushed her so far past her comfort zone, she lost control in ways she never had before at a time in her life when what she wanted was to feel like she had control again. Complicating matters was the fact that after she climbed peaks of passion she'd never even contemplated, the way he held her made her feel safe and se-cure—made her want to give herself over and let him take care of her. When she knew she needed to take care of herself. No one else could do that for her. She took another gulp of wine and met Ginger's eyes. "I'll work on it."

As Marley looked over at Ginger, Ginger's grin widened. Marley's back was to the door, so she jumped when she felt a warm hand curl around her shoulder. Turning to glance up, her eyes collided with Gage's. His lightning eyes darkened the moment they met hers. Without a word, he leaned down and took her lips in a swift kiss, his tongue stroking deeply inside. In what couldn't have been more than a few seconds, he left her flustered when he pulled away. If she doubted her control with him, all it took was one kiss and she forgot where she was. The undertow of passion was so strong between them, she felt powerless to resist it… and part of her didn't want to resist.

He turned to Ginger. "Hey Ginger, nice to see you again," he said smoothly as he slid onto the seat beside Marley.

Dazed, she wiggled over so he had room beside her. His leg rested against hers, the warm heat curling through her.

Ginger smiled brightly at Gage. "Nice to see you too! What's new at the lodge today?"

"Almost done on the inside. Don tells me he'll have the lifts running by next week. I also hired his daughter Delia to cook. I'm hoping to persuade her to help manage the front, but she says she wants to see how it goes first."

"Delia will be perfect. She was there all the time with her mom. Have you seen her since you've been home?" Ginger asked, directing her question to Marley.

"I ran into her at the store, but we barely had a chance to talk. I was with my mom, and she had her son with her." Marley glanced to Gage. "I'm so glad Don sent her your way. She worked with her mom when she got older, so she knows her way around the kitchen there. I bet she'll do great managing the front too."

Just looking at Gage flushed her again, so Marley took another quick sip of wine. The conversation moved on with Ginger offering suggestions for who to hire for cleaning and reception. As they talked, Gage rested his arm across the back of the booth, his thumb idly caressing her neck and driving her to distraction in the process. With the slightest touch, he turned her into a puddle. The current between them snapped and crackled. She lost track of the conversation though she managed to nod and make enough vague comments for Gage and Ginger to carry on.

Ginger's sharp question jolted her. "How come you didn't mention the emails to me?"

Marley swung her eyes over to Ginger and then to Gage. "I thought you'd have mentioned it to her," Gage said, holding her eyes, his gaze clear. When she didn't reply, he arched a brow in question.

Though she hadn't been purposefully withholding anything from Ginger, she felt bad she hadn't mentioned it. Gage's concern made her feel protected, which felt so good she didn't know what to do. On the heels of that came her confusion about how to rein in the feeling he elicited—the wish to simply let him take care of her.

Marley focused on Ginger again. "It's only been two emails. The second one showed up last night after you left. I didn't want to make something out of nothing." Thinking about the emails sent a curl of discomfort up her spine. She took another sip of wine. Gage's thumb kept stroking softly across the base of her neck.

Ginger chewed her lip. "What the hell? Are you worried they're connected to the robbery?"

Marley shrugged. "I don't know. They don't make any sense. Aside from my own stuff, I had nothing to do with human resources. I definitely never had any data from them for my work there."

"I've got a friend who works in private security in Seattle. He's going to trace the source of the emails and follow up with the police in Seattle," Gage interjected.

"Are you sure that's necessary? I mean, what if it's nothing?" Even though Gage had asked her about doing this, whenever she considered it, she wondered if she was over-reacting.

"If it's nothing, then it won't matter," Gage said flatly. His thumb ceased its soft strokes as his hand tightened on her shoulder. "I'm not going to sit by while you wonder who's sending those. We're also not going to let the police sleep on the investigation of the robbery."

"I'm sure they're doing everything they can. I don't want you to think you have to do this..." The part of her that savored his protectiveness bumped up against the part of her that wanted to pull the pieces of her life together on her own.

Ginger cut her off and turned to Gage, her expression somber. "Thank you for checking on this." She paused and looked at Marley. "You haven't heard from the police in weeks. Even if they mean well, they're busy and you moved away. The squeaky wheel gets the grease. If Gage has someone down there to follow up on things, maybe they'll keep digging and figure out who the hell did what they did to you. It's not okay for you to go through that and have the investigation just peter out. Gage is right, if the email thing is nothing, it won't matter what his friend finds." Ginger turned to Gage again and nodded firmly. "It means a lot to me that you're taking care of this and her. Marley'll be pissed at me for saying this, but sometimes she takes independence a little too far and never asks for help."

Marley lobbed a napkin at Ginger, but didn't have it in her to argue the point. She'd been steadily sipping her wine and had quite the buzz going. Gage glanced at her, his eyes assessing. Turning back to Ginger, he simply nodded. Their food arrived and conversation moved on. Marley couldn't think too much about the emails or the robbery because it rattled her too much. Gage's involvement unsettled her because she felt vulnerable enough as it was. But she also felt a sense of relief. He'd so easily stepped in and lifted the weight off of her, she didn't quite know what to make of it. She didn't want to get too comfortable in whatever it was between them, but it felt so good, she couldn't seem to think clearly.

Before she knew it, Gage was standing and tugging on her hand. Ginger chuckled. "You're driving her home, right?"

Marley started to protest, but Gage

shook his head. "You're not driving. I'd bet this dinner was the first thing you had to eat all day. That wine hit you hard."

He was entirely right, but she didn't want to admit it. After he'd left this morning, she'd had coffee and buried herself in working on a few apps she had in development. She tended to lose track of time when she was working like that. If it hadn't been for Ginger's call about dinner, she'd likely still be working.

She met Gage's eyes and the heat that lay banked inside whenever he was near sparked and flickered. She forced herself to focus. "Fine. I might have had a tad too much wine."

Gage gave her another tug, and she slid out of the booth. When she stood, her legs felt rubbery, and she was thankful for his strong arm clamping around her waist. Ginger stepped to her side and dropped a quick kiss on her cheek. "I'll pick you up tomorrow if you need a ride into town to pick up your car." With a smile and a wave, she was off.

Marley stood at Gage's side, savoring the delicious feel of his muscled body against hers. Gage tilted her chin up. "Ready?"

When she nodded, he reached past her to snag her purse and began walking. Marley realized how hard the wine had hit her as she realized she'd likely have lost her balance without his strong grip on her. The cold air hit her forcefully when they stepped outside. The wind kicked up and blew her hair in a swirl. She shivered as they made their way across the parking lot. When they reached his truck, she glanced up. He looked down just as she looked his way. In a flash, electricity crackled between them. Gage turned, sheltering her between his body and the truck. He took a breath, and she felt his heartbeat against her breasts. He held her gaze in the dark.

Gage brought his lips to hers, the heat of his kiss a brand. Desire thundered through her. The icy air around them was such a contrast to the heat between them, she thought she might melt. He delved deeply, his tongue tangling with hers, before he pulled back swiftly. Their breath misted in the air. He ran his hands up and down her arms. "It's freezing. Let's get you home," he said gruffly.

They drove home through the dark night, snow starting to fall, illuminated in the path of his headlights. Gage hooked his arm around her waist when they walked inside and efficiently started a fire in the woodstove before carrying her upstairs. Marley drifted into sleep, snug against his side. The moon hung low over the mountains, leaving a shimmering path on the water below.

CHAPTER 12

"Okay, what's the status on those emails?" Gage asked. He stepped around a furniture dolly in the hallway as he walked toward the office. Aidan had called him while he was in the middle of directing a crew of movers to move out the old furniture and relocate the new furniture. After Gage had attempted to persuade Don he could handle all of the moving himself, Don had simply handed him the number of a local moving company.

"I thought Navy SEALs were supposed to be smart," Don had commented.

"We like to take care of things ourselves." It chafed at Gage to pay for something as simple as lugging furniture around. He figured his relentless physical conditioning might as well come in handy where it could, so he stubbornly ignored Don and set out to move everything himself.

"You've got the funds to pay someone, don't wear yourself out moving furniture." At that, Don had walked away.

After a few hours of trudging up and down stairs by himself, Gage realized Don was smarter than he was and promptly hired someone else to do it. The last week had flown by. Delia's initial hesitance to manage the front had dissolved under the face of how much work needed to be done. She'd promptly hired cleaners and was slowly working her way through applicants for managing the reception area. After quickly discovering Gage was no help with recommendations on the menu, she'd wrangled Marley and Ginger into meeting with her to look over her ideas and offer suggestions.

Thanksgiving was days away, and Gage was due to fly down to Bellingham for one day only. He had too much to do to stay away longer and couldn't imagine being away from Marley more than that. Which should have given him pause, but he swatted away any hesitation. She'd blushed like mad when her mother stopped by to check out the progress on the lodge and invited Gage to Thanksgiving dinner. Given that Gage was either at Marley's place or she was here every day, he had enough sense to know her family would be wondering what Marley meant to him. Her mother had nodded approvingly when he'd explained he needed to see his family then since he'd be at the lodge for Christmas. He considered inviting Marley to come with him, but he sensed it was more important for her to be with her family after everything she'd been through this year.

He finally reached the office and swung the door shut behind him. "Sorry man, I missed half of what you said. I've got guys moving furniture here. I'm finally in my office."

Aidan chuckled. "No worry. I heard the racket and was talking to my receptionist here."

"So, those emails?"

"Right. When you asked me about it, I figured we might end up in a dead end. Most companies often have one internet service provider address. If anyone sent it within the company, we'd have a hard time sorting out who it was. In this case, we got lucky. The guy sent it right from his house…"

Gage cut in, anger bolting through him. "Who the hell sent it?"

"If you hadn't interrupted me, I was getting to that. Kent Walker rents the apartment where we traced the ISP address. He works at the same company Marley did. We're working on it on this end to see what else we can find on him."

Gage swore and sat down abruptly. He almost broke the phone in his hand and had to consciously ease his grip. "I'm coming down there. Let me…"

"My turn to interrupt. Hold your horses, man. Don't come down here until we have some more info. If you show up and blaze your way in to haul off and punch this guy, we may never figure out what's behind his emails. You're too emotionally involved. Let me do my job. I'll keep you up to date. Once we're ready to move, then you can come down here and be all badass."

Gage's chest was tight, anger pulsing through him. He forced himself to breath slowly. He knew Aidan was being logical, but it didn't make it any easier. "I'm not too emotionally involved."

Aidan barked a laugh. "No offense, but hell yes you are! I don't know Marley, but that woman has your number. You were one of the coolest, calmest guys on our team. You never did anything that didn't make sense even when it was damn near impossible to stay sane. You know damn well it would be stupid to show up on this guy's doorstep until we have time to figure out what's behind it. We don't even know if he had anything to do with the robbery, but I'd bet money you've already decided he did. Sit tight and wait."

Gage heard Aidan's words and knew they were rational, but the cool, calm part of himself Aidan was referring to—that part was *not* running the show when it came to Marley. The thin thread of control he had was due solely to his years of training and work as a SEAL. By virtue of habit, he'd trained impulsiveness out of his system. It took all he had not to throw his phone at the wall and ignore everything Aidan just said.

"Fuck you."

Gage could imagine Aidan's wry smile

when he replied. "Whatever, man. Let me be your friend. Don't be stupid. You've got plenty to work on at the ski lodge. Focus on that, and I'll call you as soon as I have more news."

"Fine. Don't sit on this though."

"It's at the top of my priorities. I'll call you soon," Aidan said before ending the call.

Gage sat there, staring blindly at the floor, as he tried to process what he felt. He didn't like waiting on this. His mind volleyed through an internal debate. He wanted to be driving this. *Yeah and if you weren't in so deep with Marley, you'd be running this exactly how Aidan is. He's waiting to make a move until the timing is right. You can't see straight because all you can think of is Marley.* Her green eyes flashed in his mind, and he took a gulp of air. His jaw clenched and unclenched. He stood and strode out of the office. He needed to be outside where the bracing air took his focus somewhere else.

* * *

MARLEY'S BREATH misted in the cold air as she walked along the worn trail that ran from her cabin to her parents' house. Snow crunched under her boots and occasionally fell in soft swirls when the wind blew through the trees. The trees opened onto the field beside her parents' home. Lacey stood on the deck.

"Hey Lacey!" Marley called as she began jogging to the house.

Lacey whirled around and squealed. She met Marley with a hug at the stairs.

"Hey sis! I caught the last flight out yesterday. How's it going?" Lacey hooked her arm through Marley's and pulled her along to the door.

Marley glanced at her sister, her chest tightening. Though she'd visited regularly in her years away, she hadn't realized how good it would feel to be home once and for all. Lacey's cheeks were bright from the cold. Her chestnut hair was pulled into a loose ponytail. Lacey kept her grip on Marley all the way into the kitchen where she sat down at the kitchen table with flourish. The kitchen was scented with the familiar scents of Thanksgiving and warm from the heat of the oven.

Bemused, Marley sat down across from her. Lacey grinned. "Well?"

"Well, what?"

"How's it going?" Lacey repeated.

"Pretty good."

Lacey stood and stepped to the counter. "Want some hot cider?"

"Sure. Where's Mom and Dad?"

"Mom is upstairs changing and Dad went down to pick up Don, Delia and her son. Don's truck battery froze up this morning, so Dad went to get them."

Marley nodded and took the steaming mug of hot cider Lacey carried over to her. Lacey slipped back into the chair across from her. "So, Mom says you're seeing Gage," she commented with a sly grin.

Marley fought the flush that crept up her neck, but it was useless. She shook her head. "Should've known Mom would tell you. She keeps dropping hints about how wonderful he is."

"She hardly knows anything! Oh my God, Marley! You finally have major news on the man front, and you act like nothing's happening."

Marley bit her lip to keep from laughing, but a laugh bubbled out anyway. "I'm not trying to hide anything, I just don't know where things might be going."

Lacey brushed a loose lock of hair out of her eyes. "So, what's the status with him?"

Marley chewed her lip and considered Lacey's question. The fact that she had to think about it made her uncomfortable. She toyed with the edge of a placemat and distracted herself with a sip of hot cider. Gage had been at her cabin every night straight for the last week. The nights were a blur of passion mingled with a deep comfort. It was as if she'd known Gage for far, far longer than she had. She'd come to crave the way she felt with him—alive, passionate, and deeply connected. All of this combined with the fact that he happened to be the sexiest, most beautiful man she'd ever laid eyes on resulted in her being in a befuddled daze about him when she tried to think about what they were to each other. She couldn't quite believe a man like him could want a woman like her. And yet, his body made his attraction blatantly obvious.

They didn't talk about what was happening between them. Marley's years of barely dating had been partly due to her relentless focus on work and partly due to the fact that she'd never been quite comfortable with the flirty banter that seemed to go along with making herself attractive to men. If she hadn't gotten to know Gage and seen his kindness in action, she'd have pegged him as cool and reserved. He was anything but. Yet, he didn't spell things out. He let his actions speak for themselves in every way. One of the things she loved about programming and coding was its simplicity. Once she found the path she wanted, she knew how to follow it and didn't have to wonder about the intentions of others. In relationships, it was all about wonder and wondering. She stumbled from sheer amazement about what happened between them to questions and confusion about what it all meant. To Lacey's question, she didn't quite have an answer. She didn't know if Gage considered what was happening between them serious or not. While for her, it was the deepest she'd ever gone in any relationship. She was in so far over her head, she couldn't see where to look next.

Marley took another sip of cider and met Lacey's eyes. "That's the thing. I'm not sure what our status is."

The teasing gleam faded from Lacey's eyes. "Hmm. Well, how often do you see him?"

"Every night and most days."

"Well, if that's the case, he'd better be taking this seriously. He's not some playboy, is he?"

Marley shook her head. "I don't think so. I'm just…not used to dating, or whatever you want to call this."

"Mom seems to think he's pretty awesome," Lacey said with a soft smile.

Marley chuckled. "Oh you don't need to tell me that. Ever since she stopped by the lodge to meet him, she can't stop asking about him every time we talk. I thought she was going to fall over when I told her I was seeing him."

Lacey giggled. "Let her be happy for you," she said, her eyes sobering again. "When can I meet him? I want to make sure he's a good guy. You don't need someone who's just having a little fun."

"He's flown down to Bellingham for Thanksgiving. He'll be back tomorrow afternoon. Maybe you can stop by the lodge soon. It's pretty busy up there these days."

The kitchen door opened, a gust of icy air breezing through as their father, Stan, stepped through the door with Don, Delia and Nicholas right behind him. Marley stood to give her father a hug.

"Hey girl," Stan said, squeezing her shoulder briefly before stepping away. He kicked off his boots by the door and took coats from the others.

Their mother, Holly, came downstairs into the fray and immediately got to work in the kitchen. Don sat down beside Marley and patted her shoulder.

"Good to have you home," he said softly, his voice almost drowned out by Nicholas who burst into shrieks and giggles when Stan swung him around in the air. Delia had immediately joined Holly in the kitchen, checking on the turkey and getting serving platters ready. Lacey stood up from the table and refilled her cider.

Marley met Don's eyes with a soft smile. "Good to be here. I'm glad you suggested Delia work up at the lodge. She's doing a great job, and it seems like she likes it."

Don nodded, his return smile wide. "I thought it might work out. She's been struggling with odd jobs. I'm glad Gage was willing to give her a chance."

Marley's heart tightened. Though Gage perhaps didn't know how much it meant to Don to have Last Frontier Lodge opening again and for Delia to be able to work in the place where she practically grew up, Gage's easy willingness to include them in the process meant so much for them. Gage was just…good. And it terrified her.

She forced herself off her cyclical worrying and replied to Don. "It's mutually beneficial. It's good work for Delia, and Gage doesn't know the first thing about running a kitchen like that. We could hardly get him to even look at the menus."

Don chuckled. "I thought it would be good for both of them." He paused, his eyes assessing her. "Gage is a good man. I'm glad he found you."

Marley wasn't sure she could have blushed much harder than she did. She didn't know what Gage had said to Don. Questions filled her mind, wondering if Don had some idea of what she meant to Gage. She was too abashed to ask. Before she could reply, Don patted her on the shoulder again. "Don't go worrying he said something to me, but I've been there, done that. All I have to do is see you two together, and it's plain as day. He's got it bad for you, darling, and it seems to be a two-way street. If you ask me, you two are great together. Don't let a good thing pass you by."

She started to shake her head, and Don grinned. "Not saying you were, hon. I don't hand out advice unless I think it's worth it. All I'm saying is Gage is worth it. He's on the quiet side though, so don't let that get in your way."

Still blushing madly, Marley took a quick sip of cider and nodded. She was stunned at Don's easy observation. Was it that obvious? That simple? In her mind and heart, she was tied up in knots. The only time she wasn't obsessing over how she felt and what it all meant was when she was twined bare with Gage—living and breathing in the incandescence of the sparks flying between them.

Don chuckled and changed the subject, moving on to ask her how many reservations they had for the lodge so far. She'd mentioned it to Gage a few times, but he didn't seem to be grasping that they were heading into a pretty busy few weeks. She glanced to Don again. "It's looking busy. I know you can handle it, but I'm not so sure Gage is ready for the madness."

Don nodded and shrugged. "I've got

things almost ready to roll outside, and Delia will have things lined up inside. Gage just needs to keep doing what he's doing. He's damn handy around the place. He'll be fine."

Marley grinned. "I know he will, but when I tell him we're almost booked up, all he does is nod."

"And get back to work," Don added. "He's a damn hard worker. He wanted to make this happen, and I think he will. Far as I'm concerned, Last Frontier Lodge opening up again is a damn good thing for Diamond Creek. It's personal for me, but it's gonna be a blast."

Lacey stepped back to the table, resting her hip on the edge. "I can't wait to blow down the slopes there again."

Marley glanced up at her. "You ski all the time. It's not like you've been missing out."

"Last Frontier Lodge is where we learned to ski. It's fun no matter where I go, but this'll be like old times."

Don's eyes teared up, and he stood to hug Lacey. Marley knew he'd been at loose ends to a degree since Sandy died, but Gage offering him his old job back had returned the glint to his eyes. Which made her heart clench. Gage just went about doing things that made her like him in too many ways. She batted the thought away and stood up.

The next few hours passed in a warm, familiar blur. Thanksgiving dinner was an easygoing affair in her family. Don's family had joined them off and on over the years, along with various other friends. Though they did actually sit down together at the table, the aftermath was a sprawl in the living room with a mix of sports on television, board games, and more.

Hours later, Marley walked back to her cabin with the moonlight glittering on the snow and falling in silvery shafts through the trees. She let herself inside and locked the door. It was her first night without Gage in a week, and it felt strange. She couldn't quite wrap her brain around the reality that after years of sleeping alone, a mere week with Gage and she missed his presence. He'd texted her earlier and left a message. During a brief call when it was clear he was surrounded by family based on the hum of voices in the background, her heart thrilled at his gravelly voice.

"I'll let you go. I just wanted to say good night," Marley said.

"Sorry about all the noise. My family's kind of loud."

She smiled, trying to imagine Gage, with his tendency to be reserved and quiet, in the middle of a raucous family. "It's okay. I'll see you when you get back tomorrow."

"Marley?"

"Yeah?"

There was a long pause. Gage cleared his throat. "It's just one night, but I miss you."

Marley's heart squeezed and joy spread its wings inside. "Me too."

She sat with her phone in hand for many long moments after that and fell asleep with his words endlessly repeating in her brain.

CHAPTER 13

The following morning, Marley stood at her windows, savoring the view. An eagle called nearby. As she looked around to find it, the eagle lifted from its perch on a cottonwood tree, its wings spreading wide as it flew across the field behind her cabin. She tracked the eagle's progress until it disappeared behind the trees, its shadow dark on the snow beneath it. The coffee maker beeped, and she strode into the kitchen. She stirred a dash of cream into her coffee and carried it over to her desk. She checked the fire in the woodstove and added a few logs before sitting down to get to work.

Gage was due back early this afternoon,

and she wanted to have her time free. She was picking him up at the airport in Homer. She paused to look out the window. She'd set her desk up so it faced the view. The morning sun was filtered through the haze from a foggy, cold morning. Shafts broke through and fell on the bay. The water was calm this morning. A raven called with magpies chattering in response. A stellar jay squawked and landed on the railing outside the window, it's blue and black coloring bright in the foggy, gray morning.

She took a breath and opened her laptop. She quickly got to work checking on the reservations for the lodge and then moving on to work on other projects. Her email beeped. When she pulled it up, another email from the unknown person in human resources sat there. It looked so innocuous, but her chest tightened and anxiety swirled in her belly. This email was still vague, again asking about the flash drive and reminding her she was obligated to return all company property. The only addition was a specific warning that she was required to respond.

She immediately closed her laptop and pushed her chair back. She grabbed her mug of coffee and took a sip. The warmth anchored her, but she'd lost focus and knew trying to work would be a waste of time. The temptation to read and re-read the latest email would tug at her every second she was on the computer. She looked around for her phone. Spying it on the kitchen counter, she stood and snatched it up, immediately calling Ginger.

A while later, she walked into Misty Mountain Café. She perused the chalkboard specials while she waited in line. Once she had a coffee and sandwich, she snagged a table in the corner. The café was bustling with a low hum of conversation and music. Ginger entered moments later and joined her.

"Hey you!" Ginger exclaimed, giving Marley a quick hug before sitting down. She pushed her hood back and smoothed her glossy brown hair. "It's freezing out! I wasn't ready for winter yet."

"Technically, it's not winter for another few weeks."

Ginger rolled her eyes. "As far as I'm concerned, it's winter even if winter solstice hasn't happened yet. It's been below freezing every day all week and there's snow on the ground."

Marley chuckled. "I know. I'm loving it, actually. Seattle weather was rainy all winter and never got cold enough for me to appreciate the contrast when it was warmer."

Ginger tilted her head. "Okay, whatever works. I like winter, but that doesn't mean I won't complain about the cold. Having Last Frontier Lodge open again will make winter so much more fun around here. Any word on the official opening date?"

Marley shook her head. "Not a precise date. I set the booking dates to start the day after Christmas. I suggested to Gage that he maybe have a local opening day before the hotel has guests, but he hasn't confirmed anything yet. Don told me to stop worrying about it."

Ginger giggled. "You're a world class worrier. Speaking of that, you mentioned you had another email. Have you talked to Gage about it?"

"It just showed up this morning, and he's flying back to Alaska as we speak. I'm not sure what he can do about it. I think maybe I'm making more of it than I should. Maybe I should just reply and tell them I don't know what the hell they're talking about."

Ginger shook her head forcefully, her hair swinging. "No, you shouldn't. Gage said he asked his friend to look into them, so wait and see. When will he be back?"

"This afternoon. I'm picking him up at the airport in Homer."

Ginger arched a brow, her blue eyes taking on a gleam. "So we're at the 'picking up from the airport' stage then?"

"That's a stage?"

Marley felt so out of her depth with relationships in general, and more so with Gage. Her last relationship that comprised more than a few dates was in college and wasn't particularly memorable.

Ginger's eyes sobered. "I'm teasing, Marley. I can tell just by looking at you, you're overthinking this thing with Gage. He's a good guy, and he really likes you. How about you try to enjoy what's happening?"

"Easy for you to say," Marley retorted.

Ginger set her coffee down. "No, it's not easy for me to say. While you've been busy with work, I married my college sweetheart and watched it fall apart. It was awful, and I never want to repeat the experience. But I'm not going to give up just because I'm scared to death. I'm the first person to be skeptical of a good thing, but I think Gage is a good guy, and he happens to like you. He can hardly keep his eyes off of you. I can't say I know what will happen, but I don't think he's planning to screw you over."

Marley reached over and squeezed Ginger's hand. "I'm sorry. I didn't mean to sound dismissive. I know it was a nightmare when things blew up with Tony."

Ginger shook her head. "I know you do. I wasn't bringing that up to make you feel bad, just to say that I get it. Letting go and trying to trust someone else can be terrifying, so I completely understand why it might be hard for you. But I don't want you to get so worked up you don't even give yourself a chance."

Marley nodded. "I'm out of practice with dating, if that's what we're doing. It's even worse because Gage is some fantasy guy. I mean, he's sexy as hell, he's nice, and he used to be a Navy SEAL! I'm just a nerdy girl."

"I'll give it to you that Gage is some kind of something, but you act like you're not a catch. You're gorgeous and smart as hell. You've kept your nose buried so deep in books and computers, you've never bothered to notice you could have had your pick of guys."

Marley flushed. "Okay, whatever you say. Meanwhile, I'll try to stop worrying. It would be much easier if these emails didn't randomly show up out of nowhere."

"That's why you're going to wait and see what Gage's friend has to say," Ginger said firmly. "Have you talked to your parents about it?"

Marley shook her head. "No! I don't want them to worry."

Ginger nodded. "Okay, but I hope you're going to talk to them if this keeps up."

"I'm hoping we can figure out who's sending them and sort it out first. They'll be beside themselves. They finally stopped calling me every day."

Marley was frustrated with the emergence of these emails, which had her worried and didn't make sense. Whenever she tried to convince herself they were nothing, her gut would blare loudly. Her parents had been so worried after the robbery. They'd had flown to Seattle and stayed with her for a week and only stopped with daily calls after she moved back to Diamond Creek. She understood why they'd hovered so, but it made her feel helpless and vulnerable.

Ginger met her gaze and nodded. "Got it. I'm just glad you let me know."

Conversation moved on to lighter matters. By the time Marley left the café, snow was floating from the sky, and she had just enough time to get to Homer to meet Gage's flight. It didn't appear it would amount to much, but she was glad Gage would be in before nightfall. As she drove south toward Homer, she took in the familiar view. The Sterling Highway hugged the coastline of the Kenai Peninsula, which offered vista upon vista of stunning views. The mountains across Kachemak Bay stood tall and snowy against the sky. The green of the spruce forest was bright in the gray, snowy afternoon. As she drove past a clearing among the trees, she saw a pair of moose nibbling on alder. She stopped to watch them. She'd missed seeing wildlife while she lived away from Alaska. Moose here were a common sight, gangly and elegant at once. The pair turned to look at her car when she pulled over. Snow fell softly upon them as they looked away and continued eating.

When she pulled up at the airport in

Homer, the plane she presumed to be Gage's was landing. She parked and quickly walked into the small airport. She watched as Gage walked down the steps of the small plane. Her heart caught in her throat, and her pulse quickened. Even at a distance, he was all man. He moved with efficiency, his broad shoulders filling out his lightweight jacket, his strong arms swinging. Though he was clearly on the move, he paused and held the door for an elderly couple, lifting the bag out of the older man's hands and carrying it.

His eyes met hers as soon as he stepped inside. It was as if there was a magnetic pull between them. She could barely hold herself back from running to him. He nodded toward the couple beside him, lifting the small bag he carried for them. She walked to meet them, her body vibrating at the thrill of seeing him. *For God's sake, Marley. He was only gone for one night.* She ignored her internal talk and leaned up to kiss him.

His lips were chilled from the cool air outside. He tugged her to his side with his free arm. "Hey there." His gray eyes held hers, flashing like lightning. "Let me carry this outside, and then we can get my bag," he said, gesturing to the small bag in his hand.

The man turned to him. "You don't need to do that. I can get it."

The older couple held on to each other, appearing to need each other's support to walk. Gage shook his head. "Just tell me where you're going, and I'll carry it."

The woman smiled. "You're a good boy. We're calling a cab, so if you'll walk it over to the waiting area, we'll be fine."

Marley followed them over, Gage holding her close every step of the way. After making sure the couple was settled on a bench, Gage turned and glanced around. He quickly pulled her into the short hallway that led to the restrooms.

"Hey…"

He cut her greeting off with a kiss, his lips claiming hers fiercely. He backed her against the wall, leaning one elbow against the wall while his free hand cupped her face. The banked heat that had flickered the moment she saw Gage soared to life, engulfing her in its heat. Her core drew tight and pleasure twirled through her. Their kiss went from hot to searing with Gage's tongue sweeping inside her mouth. He stroked his thumb down her neck, dusting over her pulse. She was instantly wet, desperate for more. She gasped in his mouth, frantically sliding her hands inside his jacket. He shifted his weight, his knee sliding between her thighs. Pleasure spiked when his knee brushed against her. She lost sense of where they were. All she knew was Gage was here with her again, and she couldn't get close enough.

Suddenly, he tore his lips away and swore. His breath was ragged, matching hers. She met his eyes, smoky and intent on hers. His palm was curled around her breast, her heart beating rapidly against the heat of his touch. He took a deep breath and stepped back an inch, his hand sliding down to curl around her waist. It felt like a chasm opened between them.

"I just wanted to kiss you, but... We don't have much privacy here, and I can't seem to keep my hands to myself when it comes to you."

The sounds of the airport filtered into her awareness. A flush washed through her. She bit her lip and glanced around. They were blessedly out of sight, but at any second, someone could turn into the hallway. When she met his eyes again, his mouth curled at the corner. "Let's get my bag and get out of here."

Gage stepped back, grabbing her hand as he did, and turned to walk toward the small baggage area. After a short wait, they walked out to her car and she started driving back to Diamond Creek. The snow fell lazily, floating past the windows and sliding across the windshield when it landed. Marley felt warm inside and out when Gage reached across the console, his palm curling around her thigh, its heat traveling straight to her heart.

* * *

GAGE RELAXED inside for the first time since Marley had dropped him off at the airport yesterday morning. He loved his family and enjoyed Thanksgiving with them, but he hadn't been able to stop thinking about Marley. His thoughts bounced between missing her, wishing she were there with him, and worrying about her. He glanced over, taking in her auburn hair falling loosely around her shoulders, the freckles sprinkled on her nose and cheeks, and her forest green eyes. He'd almost lost control in the airport, ready to tear her clothes off and take her right there. An iron grip on his impulses was a huge part of the reason he'd become a Navy SEAL. Marley made him question his ability to manage his impulses because when it came to her, his control was weak. He forced himself to look away, watching the mountains roll by, and wondered what to do with his feelings. He was a planner, and Marley had come out of nowhere. Disoriented as he was, he couldn't consider not being around her, so he'd have to figure out how to regain control.

Gage walked down one of the halls at the lodge, marveling at how much the place had been transformed with a thorough cleaning and new furnishings. Marley had insisted he formally pick an opening date, so he'd finally selected the day after Christmas as the first day the slopes would be open. As much as he wanted this, the reality of his dream was hurtling toward him so fast he couldn't quite catch up. Marley had shown him the reservation list, and he'd choked on his coffee. If it weren't for Marley's work on the website, Don's steady and able help, and Delia's energy and enthusiasm, he'd feel lost.

His phone buzzed. He tugged it out of

his pocket. "Gage, here."

"Hey man," Aidan replied. "Do you have a minute?"

Gage picked up his pace on the way back to his office. "Yup. What do you have for me?" He passed through the reception area and kitchen, and kicked his office door shut behind him.

"Kent Walker has something to hide. We know that much. What we don't know is what," Aidan said.

"He's the guy behind the emails, right?"

"Yup. Once we traced those emails to him, I set one of my guys to work on monitoring his account. Kent's an accountant and handles the accounts for the company Marley used to work for, along with a few others. My hunch is that whatever he thinks Marley has doesn't have anything to do with human resources. I've talked to the detective handling the investigation related to the robbery down here, and he took what we had and got a warrant signed off for surveillance on his online activities. We're cleared to keep monitoring for now. I think it's time for you to ask Marley how she knew this guy and what she might have accidentally stumbled upon."

Gage forced himself to take a slow breath. He was doing his damnedest to let Aidan handle this, but being so far away in Alaska chafed at Gage. He was also constantly battling his fury at whoever lay behind the robbery and now this. His gut told him they were connected. His brain reminded him he needed to let Aidan do what he did best. Much as Gage wanted to strong-arm this investigation, he knew it wouldn't help. But when it came to Marley, reason had to fight to be heard in his brain.

"I don't want to scare her, but I don't see any other way to find out how she knew this guy," Gage said tightly.

"Me neither. Talk to her when you can and let me know what she says." Aidan paused before continuing. "I'm betting you're ready to run down here. Don't," he said flatly.

Gage gritted his teeth. "Right. I'll wait, but keep me in the loop."

"You got it."

The line went dead in Gage's ear. He slipped the phone back in his pocket and stared out the window. Spruce trees marched up the hill behind the lodge, flanking the ski slopes. Snow was gradually accumulating. Don predicted they'd have more than enough before Christmas. Gage rested a hand on the window frame and tried to rein in his anger. He wanted answers and fast. He knew he needed to talk to Marley about what Aidan had turned up, but he didn't want to rattle her. He kept recalling the look in her eyes the night he'd shown up unexpectedly. He turned away from the window, battening down his feelings. He spent the rest of the afternoon immersed in work, dogging Don's steps as he showed Gage how to run the lifts. An afternoon outside with the icy breeze whipping at him kept his mind occupied and off of the disconcerting feelings Marley brought up.

* * *

MARLEY PUSHED AWAY from her desk and stood up for a stretch. She'd been at work most of the day tweaking the code on an app she'd sent out to a few friends for beta testing. When she'd leapt into the world of software and applications development after college, she'd been willing to try anything. She was damn good at writing code, so she'd bounced through a few jobs before settling at the last place she worked for almost seven years. Among other things, they developed games to help with training for the health field. If someone had asked her if she'd love doing that before she did it, she'd have been doubtful. She'd quickly learned that she became immersed in the task of finding ways to make learning fun and engaging. She'd worried when she left her job that she might struggle to get her footing on her own. While she had a steep learning curve as far as the business end of things, she was already discovering that health companies she'd partnered with before were thrilled to hear from her. She had the benefit of not needing a ton of income to meet her meager expenses, so it looked as if she'd be working for herself steadily with freelance development work within the next few months.

Her phone beeped insistently, and she snagged it off her desk. "Hello."

"Hi Marley, it's Kent Walker."

"Oh, uh, hey Kent. What's up?"

Kent worked in accounting at the same company she'd worked for in Seattle. He was a step beyond an acquaintance, but they'd never been particularly friendly either. He'd dated a friend of hers from work who used to take care of her apartment whenever she was out of town. Not that there was much to take care of, but she had a few plants that needed watering. Becky had lived in the same apartment building, so she'd volunteered. Marley returned the favor in kind and fed her cats when Becky was out of town. Marley would occasionally encounter Becky and Kent on the elevator in their building. Beyond those brief encounters, Marley barely knew Kent. She didn't know how he had her number, or why he would be calling. Tension coiled inside.

"I'm following up on a few emails human resources sent to you. No big deal, but you need to get back to them. Thought I'd do you a favor and give you a heads up on it."

The knot of tension coiled tighter inside. Marley may not have known Kent well, but as far as she knew, his work in accounting had nothing to do with HR. She fought the urge to tell him she didn't have what they kept asking her about and beat back the questions that welled inside.

"Marley?"

"I'm here. I guess...thanks for the heads up," she finally said.

Kent cleared his throat in the following pause. "Make sure you get in touch with HR, okay?"

"Sure. Thanks for calling." Marley ended the call before Kent had a chance to say anything else. She stared at the phone in her hand, as if it would tell her why he'd really called and what he had to do with the mysterious emails. Her heart beat rapidly, and she felt slightly nauseous. She pulled up Becky's number in her contacts, her index finger hovering over it as she considered whether to call her. She abruptly decided against it. She didn't even know if Kent and Becky were still on good terms. Their dating had been on and off. She and Becky weren't close enough for Marley to know much more than the surface details. If she called Becky and started asking questions, that would only tip Kent off. She couldn't stop wondering what was on those flash drives and why it was so damn important.

With a sigh, she tossed her phone on the kitchen counter and stalked over to the windows. The morning had dawned cold, windy and overcast. The sun had never shown itself. Its hidden light was already fading behind the thick veil of clouds. Restless, Marley grabbed her jacket and tugged her boots on. She started walking and quickly noticed she'd automatically headed along one of the trails that cut through the woods to Last Frontier Lodge. She'd unconsciously sought out Gage. She picked up her pace. The wind came in icy gusts, chilling her through. Once she reached the edge of one of the ski slopes, she stayed by the trees and made her way to the lodge. The light was fading faster than she'd considered.

When she began climbing up the back steps, the outside lights came on and the door swung open. Gage stood inside the door, his hard-muscled form filling the doorway. Her breath caught in her throat. Relief washed over her. She didn't like to think about it, but she was on edge. She'd finally started to settle a tiny bit after coming home and getting away from the apartment where she'd been robbed and attacked. She'd discovered how fragile her hold on her anxiety had been when the emails started. The call from Kent today had keyed her up even further. The sight of Gage was so good, she almost ran across the deck. His teeth flashed with his smile in the dusky light.

"Thought that was you," he said as he stood aside and gestured for her to come in.

Marley stepped inside, shivering from the cold. The door Gage opened led into a hallway adjacent to the lodge kitchen, which was bustling with activity. Gage turned to her when he closed the door, his pewter gaze coasting over her face. He wore jeans, hanging low on his hips, and another one of his worn t-shirts that stretched across his sculpted chest. It was ridiculous how sexy he was. His chocolate brown hair was rumpled, as if he'd run his hand through it a few too many times. Marley's pulse quickened, and her belly fluttered—a semi-permanent state when she was near him.

His eyes darkened a shade, that smoky gaze sending desire sliding through her veins. He reached for her hands, the warmth from his bringing a sigh to her lips.

"You're freezing," he said.

"I forgot my gloves when I started walking over here."

His mouth kicked up in a grin. "You coulda called me. I'd have come to get you."

"I didn't really think about it. I just

started walking…and ended up here." When she spoke, she recalled her restlessness and the reason behind it.

Gage's eyes coasted over her face. "Everything okay?"

She shrugged. "I, uh…"

She paused when something clattered in the kitchen. Gage glanced over his shoulder and back to her. "Come on. Let's get you where it's warmer. Delia will insist you have something hot to drink. Then you're telling me what's on your mind."

Marley met his eyes in the dim light in the hallway. He knew her better than she'd like to think. She nodded and let him lead her into the kitchen. Delia had transformed it from the sterile, quiet space it had been into a bustling, lively kitchen. While there were a few weeks left between now and Christmas, Delia had hired a crew and was doing practice runs for the locals on invitation only nights. When Marley had heard this, she'd been impressed. Delia had explained she needed some way to make sure the kitchen staff had enough practice with the menu and were ready for busy nights. Marley's mother had already attended the first two and could hardly shut up about it.

Delia turned their way when they walked into the kitchen. "Hey Marley! Gage said he thought he saw you walking over. How's it going?" Delia carefully measured flour and added it to a mixing bowl. "We're working on the baked goods for the menu," Delia explained as she gestured for a young woman nearby to pass her some spices. Delia added a few spices to whatever she was working on and wiped her hands on her apron. "Let me get you something. We have tea, hot cider and cocoa. Take your pick."

After Delia poured Marley a large steaming mug of fresh hot cider, she shooed them out of the kitchen. Gage led the way down an unfamiliar hallway and up a flight of stairs. Marley quickly realized they were entering a living space separated from the rest of the hotel and discovered his grandparents had created a charming private apartment that occupied the upper floor over the kitchen and restaurant. The living area had an open living room and kitchen, which overlooked the ski slopes to one side and offered a view of Kachemak Bay in the corner. Moonlight haloed through the clouds, leaving a smudged streak of light on the bay. The slopes were barely visible in the falling darkness.

Gage gave her a quick tour. Beyond the common area, there was a short hallway with two small bedrooms, a bathroom, and a large master suite with its own private bath. It didn't appear as if Gage had personalized the space. When he caught her glancing around, he shrugged sheepishly. "I've been so busy working on the lodge, I haven't taken any time to decorate in here. My grandmother must have cleared out all of her personal furniture because it was empty when I got here. What you see is stuff I hauled up here from some of the rooms. My sisters say they'll be up here over the holidays to help out."

Marley bit back her grin. "Well, you did say decorating wasn't your thing. Maybe I can help with that too."

He nodded with alacrity. "You can do whatever you want. I'd like to make it nicer. I keep thinking I should invite you over here, but as you can see, your place is a little homier."

Marley giggled, soft warmth suffusing her at the idea of Gage thinking about having her over and worrying what she might think. Anxiety rose behind that feeling because she still didn't quite know where things were headed with him. It was hard to reconcile the eagerness of her heart and body with her mind's frequent reminders to take things slow and not overthink what was happening. She took a breath and followed him back down the short hallway to the living room. The couch looked as if it had come from the reception area. She sat down, tucking her feet under her and curling her hands around the warm mug of cider. When she took a sip, she realized she'd need to take it slow. Delia didn't mess around with her cider and it had quite a kick. Gage had helped himself as well and quickly took a swallow before turning to her, his eyes instantly serious.

"Okay, what made you walk through the woods when it was almost dark?" Gage asked bluntly.

Marley started to shrug when Gage arched a brow and shook his head. She bit her lip and looked away. She didn't want to feel the way she had since the robbery—anxious, hyper-vigilant, and humming with a thread of unease. She didn't want to seem helpless and needy with Gage. But dammit, he was too perceptive. She sighed and met his eyes, figuring it would be pointless to avoid telling him about the call because she'd eventually tell him. "A guy from my old job called a little bit ago…"

Gage interjected. "What did he want?" he asked quickly, his eyes sharpening.

"I was getting to that. He said he was giving me a heads up that I needed to get back to HR about the emails. He made it seem like he was trying to do me a favor. I don't know what he has to do with any of it, or why he'd call. We weren't really friends. He dated a woman from work who lived in my apartment building. I don't know what to think."

As soon as she explained, she felt silly. It was just a phone call.

"What's his name?"

"Kent Walker."

Gage's hand tightened on the armrest. His expression was carefully controlled. "Right. Well, I planned to ask you if you knew him."

"What?!" The back of her neck prickled. Her unease grew by leaps and bounds. If Gage planned to ask her if she knew Kent, that could only mean he somehow knew who Kent was and had reason to wonder about her connection to him. Which frightened her. "How do you know who Kent is?"

Gage cleared his throat. "My friend in security traced those emails back to him. Aidan followed up with the police working on the investigation for your robbery, and they got a warrant for him to keep monitoring Kent's emails. He asked me this morning to find out how you knew Kent. We know he worked at the same company as you did. Aidan doesn't have much more to offer, other than that Kent handles accounting for several businesses." Gage paused and swore under his breath.

Anxiety knotted in her chest. She didn't understand why Kent would send those emails and what he wanted. "I don't understand. I don't know what he's doing. I..."

Gage held her gaze, his expression hard to read. "We need to know the extent of your contacts with him. It may not be obvious at first, but break it down for me. How long did you know him, how often did you see him, that kind of thing."

Marley swallowed through the tight feeling in her chest and throat. "That's the thing. I didn't really know him well. Just like you said, he handled accounts. I worked in development. He dated Becky, a woman from work who lived in my apartment building. I'd sometimes see them in the halls or on the elevator. I didn't even know he had my number."

Gage nodded slowly. "How close were you and Becky?"

Marley shrugged. "We were friendly, but not too close. I worked almost all the time. One time when she went on vacation, she asked me to check on her cats since we lived in the same building. After that, she'd water my plants whenever I was gone, which wasn't often really. That's it."

"Did she have a key to your apartment?"

"I gave her a spare whenever I went out of town, but she always returned it. I thought about calling her, but now I'm not sure. Kent's call seemed weird. I got freaked out, and then I thought it was silly. But if he's the one who sent me those emails..." She paused and took a breath. She thought she'd closed the door on the robbery when she moved home. She wasn't silly enough to think she would simply forget what hap-pened. But she thought that by finally going home to Diamond Creek, she'd be able to get a grip on the fears that dominated her life in the days and weeks after the robbery, and perhaps she'd manage to sleep through the night again. Those stupid emails sent a prickle of unease through her. She hadn't wanted to connect them to the robbery, but something felt strange. Kent's call and learning he'd been the one to send the emails stirred the anxiety she'd kept at bay for the last few months.

She'd finally slept all the way through the night a few times when Gage was with her, and now her anxiety had notched up again with her stomach knotted and tension coiled throughout her body. She took a slow breath, focusing on the heat from her mug of hot cider. She felt Gage's palm slide slowly across her shoulder to rest on the back of her neck. He squeezed gently, subtly easing the cords of tension in her shoulders and neck.

"I don't know what to do. This makes me tired," she whispered. Tears pricked at the back of her eyes. She took a swallow of cider, savoring the burn from the alcohol that came with it.

"No one is going to hurt you again. That much, I can promise you. I won't tell you not to worry because that would be a waste of breath. Aidan's working with the police down there, and we'll get to the bottom of this. In the meantime, you're either staying with me every night, or I'm staying at your place. If you don't mind, that is." Gage's words were soft and gravelly. His hand kept subtly massaging her neck.

Part of Marley wanted to wrap herself in the comfort he offered, but she needed to be able to handle this herself. She wanted to right the ship of her life herself, but she was weary and Gage's strength tugged at her, made her want to let go. She took another gulp of cider and glanced up at him. His eyes locked to hers. She lost herself in the stormy, smoky gray of his eyes and forgot the internal push and pull of her own mind. His hand moved away from her neck when he carefully brushed a loose curl out of her eyes, tucking the wayward lock of hair behind her ear. His touch sent shivers through her. It occurred to her that she hadn't replied to him yet. "I don't mind," she said softly.

He looked puzzled.

"Staying with you every night," she added.

The corner of his mouth kicked up. His eyes darkened, skating over her face. "We're going to get to the bottom of this. Do you mind if I call Aidan right now? I'd rather let him know sooner rather than later about Kent's call."

Marley shook her head. Gage shifted his hips and pulled his phone out of his pocket. His free hand idly stroked through her hair as he waited for Aidan to answer. She barely focused on what he said to Aidan, her body on high alert. Gage's soft touch was like sparks on the tinder of her desire. After a few more minutes, Gage set his phone down.

"Aidan's going to follow up with the police tomorrow." He paused and turned to her. "It's killing me not to be down there handling this."

Marley shook her head sharply. "No! Don't do that." Her words tumbled out rapidly. She tried to make sense of her responses. She wanted this all to go away, wanted to handle it herself, but she couldn't seem to resist Gage's protectiveness. It was a muddle and trying to sort through it only tired her. The mere thought of Seattle sent a wave of fear crashing through her. She couldn't stand to think of Gage not being here. With her. A single night without him had been too much. *You're in too deep. You don't even know what he wants from this.* She ignored the voice of reason in her mind. All she knew was she felt safe when Gage was with her…and so much more.

"I'm not going anywhere. Even though I'd prefer to be more hands on, I trust Aidan completely. He'll keep us in the loop every step of the way. It just makes me sick this guy is messing with you. I'd love to go down there and make him regret it," Gage nearly growled.

His words washed through her. The part of her that wasn't fighting against the tide of feeling savored the warmth and security she felt with him. She tried to summon reason, but she didn't have it in her just now. She looked up, her eyes colliding with his intense gaze. She couldn't form words as sensation whipped through her. She felt the pull of his gaze from the inside out. Her core drew tight with need. He reached for the mug of cider in her hands and deliberately removed it, carefully setting it on the table beside the couch, his eyes never leaving hers. He said her name, his voice rough and raw. Her pulse raced. The moment held still between them, the delicious ache of want building to a fervor in the quiet. The low charge between them hummed and arced higher. In a swift movement, Gage's lips crashed against hers, and she dove headlong into the tornado of sensation swirling around and within them.

The fear and anxiety that had run on high idle since the phone call earlier spiraled into a frenzy of heated desire. Marley couldn't get close enough fast enough. Gage's kiss consumed her—wet, scorching and overpowering. His tongue swept in commanding strokes, tangling with hers before he pulled away, tugging at her bottom lip before his lips, tongue and teeth left a searing trail down the side of her neck. He caught her earlobe in his teeth, eliciting deep shivers throughout her body. Need coiled tightly inside of her and she tore at his clothes, sighing with relief when she could run her hands over the muscled planes of his chest and his rock hard abs. He shoved her shirt up and over her head. She straddled him, savoring the hard, heated length of him against the core of her.

He placed a palm on her chest, levering

her back slightly. She lifted her eyes to meet his hooded gaze—dark smoke caressed her. In slow motion, he eased his thumb under the clasp of her bra. With the barest motion, the clasp gave way, her aching breasts tumbling free. He breathed her name as his hands cupped her breasts. She sighed at his touch, achy shivers racing through her. He tugged at her nipples, pinching them lightly before his mouth closed over one and then the other, laving them, dragging his fingers in lazy circles through the moisture left behind from his mouth.

Marley shifted back and tore at the buttons on his jeans, curling her hand around his arousal. Gage's breath hissed through his teeth. She stood and yanked at his jeans until they fell around his ankles. He kicked them away and reached for her. Ignoring him, she slid her hands up his thighs and gripped his briefs. With a swift pull, they followed the course of his jeans, his kick landing them in another corner of the room. Again, he reached for her. Again, she ignored him. She'd come to learn he was unabashedly comfortable in his nakedness. It was no wonder given that his body was a work of art—all hard muscles and lean glory. He bore a few scars, including one that curled in a jagged line on his side and around to his back. She meant to ask about it, but now wasn't the time. She curled her hand around the velvet length of his cock. His head fell back with a groan.

She knelt between his knees and took him in her mouth. His cock pulsed when she pushed down, bringing him fully into her mouth. She settled in to enjoy driving him to the brink. She dragged her tongue up, down and around his cock. She brought him into her mouth again and again, stroking, licking and sucking. She curled her hand around his wet length as she moved up and down. With a guttural cry, he pushed her back, pulling her to standing. He took her mouth in another overpowering kiss, his hands roaming over her body. He shoved her jeans down over her hips, his hands roughly cupping her bottom and pulling her against his arousal.

He tore his lips from hers, turning her in his arms. His hands curled under her breasts from behind as he nipped her neck. Her hips moved reflexively back, need clawing through her. She still wore her panties, the feel of his heated shaft through the black silk ratcheted up the liquid heat spiraling inside. His hand traveled down her abdomen and cupped her mound through the silk, damp from her desire. The stroke of his roughened skin against the silk brought her rapidly to the edge. His touch, rough and soft at once, coaxed her closer and closer as he dragged his fingers back and forth over the silk between her thighs. Desperation built as she clung to the delicious edge.

Her knees gave way and she fell against the couch. She felt him fumble and then swear and go still. Marley glanced over her shoulder. His expression bordered on pain. "Thought I had a condom."

"I'm on the pill. There's nothing to worry about either…I trust you."

Gage stared at her. The moment lengthened, and she began to wish she hadn't spoken. He cleared his throat. "Are you sure?"

She turned again and held his eyes. When she nodded, he closed his eyes and his shoulders rose and fell with a deep breath. When he opened them again, his gaze burned into her.

He hooked a finger over her panties and dragged them down. Before she could speak, his knelt behind her and slid his fingers into her wet seam. A ragged moan fell from her as he stroked through her folds and dove into her channel, stretching her. His mouth joined his fingers, exploring every inch of her hot, wet core. Tremors built and heat twisted inside. She teetered on the edge of delicious madness.

He suddenly stood, his fingers slowly sliding out of her. She felt the hot brush of his shaft against her, barely nudging at her entrance. He held still for an electric moment. She quivered and pushed her hips back. Suddenly, she felt the lush surge of his cock as it filled her. He sank to the hilt, seating himself deeply inside her slick channel. One of his hands curled around her hip as he began to move while the other slid up her back, threading into her hair.

He established a steady rhythm, stretching her and filling her deeply again and again and again. Sensation took over. Marley didn't know where her body ended and his began. All she knew was that she wanted more, her hips slamming back to meet his. Feverish need suffused her as she throbbed around him. She raced toward the ecstasy her body craved. His hand slipped between her thighs, his thumb caressing the center of her desire. Pleasure stormed through her as she flew apart, the only thing holding her up his strong embrace as he surged inside once more with a guttural cry. Shudders rippled through her. His hand loosened in her hair, sliding slowly down her back to rest in the small arch. Ragged breathing echoed in the room. She felt him relax against her before he slowly pulled out. She collapsed on the couch, her heart still pounding, pulses of her orgasm lingering.

He deftly lifted her in his arms. She was discovering he appeared to enjoy carrying her around. Though she'd never been one to think much of that, she savored it—the feeling of giving herself over to his strength. He strode quickly down the hallway into the bedroom. Though it was spare of decoration, his bed was piled high with pillows and a thick down quilt. He climbed in with her in his arms. She rested against his side, her head tucked into his shoulder. The cool sheets brought a shiver. His warm palm stroked up and down her back in slow circles.

CHAPTER 15

Marley slid into the booth across from Lacey who looked up from the menu she was perusing with a grin. "Hey! Can you believe it? I'm early!"

Marley giggled. "I noticed, what's gotten into you?"

Lacey tucked a lock of chestnut hair behind her ear. "I've been craving pizza for days and I needed my Marley fix."

They were meeting for lunch at Glacier Pizza, a longstanding restaurant in Diamond Creek and a local favorite. Marley glanced around and felt a sense of comfort steal over her. Glacier Pizza had barely changed over the years beyond creative additions to its menu. The restaurant was simple, low on frills and produced amazing pizza. Marley and Lacey had spent time here regularly when they were younger. Lacey had called this morning and demanded Marley meet her for lunch.

Marley met Lacey's smiling green eyes. "It's freezing out and pizza is perfect. So what's up?"

Lacey shrugged. "Not much. I'm trying to decide what to do for the rest of winter."

"Don't you have some guiding trips planned?"

"Last winter, I signed on to lead a few trips through an outfit in Anchorage, but it's rough in the winter. It's too damn cold. I'm thinking about starting a small business here where I coordinate trips for others, but only lead a few myself every summer. What do you think?"

Marley squealed. "I think it's perfect! You've always blown me away with what a badass you are, but sometimes I worry about you. I know Mom and Dad will be relieved you don't plan to keep guiding in the winter."

Lacey grinned and rolled her eyes. "I know they worry. I'll always do some because I can't stand not being outside for most of the summer." She paused, her usually confident gaze looking uncertain. "Do you think maybe you could help me come up with a website and stuff like that? With your business and tech experience, you know what you're doing. I definitely don't."

"Of course! Whatever I can do to help, I'll be glad to do. When are you thinking of getting this up and running?"

"I was thinking if I did some planning this winter, I could maybe start next summer. Do you think I have enough time?"

Marley was so unaccustomed to seeing Lacey uncertain about anything, it was endearing. She grinned. "Sis, you're already doing all of it. You're just talking about being the one to make it happen. You can pull it off."

Lacey's eyes flashed with her grin. "If you say so. So, what's up at Last Frontier Lodge? Mom said she's been up for every local's dinner that Delia's hosted, and they're amazing."

"Delia's doing a great job. The lodge is on track to open the day after Christmas. We have reservations almost completely booked from then all the way to the middle of January." Marley couldn't help the thrill of pride she felt. Gage was making his childhood dream a reality.

"We?" Lacey asked with a gleam in her eyes.

Marley flushed straight through. Their waiter arrived in time for her to gather herself. After they ordered, Lacey eyed her. "Don't think you're getting off the hook. Give me the goods on what's going on with you and Gage."

Marley sighed, fighting the blush that raced up her neck and face again. "Things are…going."

Lacey rolled her eyes. "That doesn't tell me anything."

"Okay, okay. I don't know. I guess we're together. I just wish I knew what that meant. I'm horrible at the relationship thing. I mean, I see him every night and I need to figure out how to ask him what he thinks of us, but I don't know how."

Lacey's teasing gaze sobered. "Well, how serious are you about him?"

Marley's heart gave a hard thump. She'd been trying so hard *not* to think about how she felt deep down, but she was starting to worry that might be a bad plan. Beyond mind-blowing sex, Gage had crawled through the cracks of her defenses with his protectiveness, his warmth, and his kindness to everyone around him.

Marley met Lacey's eyes and sighed. "I guess it's pretty serious. Gage is…well, you'd have to be around him a bit to see it, but he's a really good guy." As Marley expounded, she eventually got to the part about his help with the issues around the emails and the investigation into the robbery in Seattle, completely forgetting she hadn't told Lacey about it.

Lacey's eyes widened. "What do you mean? How come you haven't mentioned this to me? Mom and Dad are going to want to know too."

Marley silently swore. She'd purposefully not been talking about it with her family so they wouldn't worry. They'd already been through enough worry over her the last few months. "Lacey, I don't want Mom and Dad to worry. I'm sorry I didn't tell you sooner, but please don't tell them. I'm fine. Gage is with me every night. His friend works in security in Seattle and is coordinating with the police on it."

Their conversation paused when their

pizza arrived. After the waiter moved on, Lacey eyed her, her expression hurt. "I understand why you don't want Mom and Dad to worry, but maybe you could've let me know what's going on."

Marley felt a wash of guilt. She hadn't purposefully been keeping this from Lacey, but she'd grown so accustomed to handling things on her own, she hadn't reached out to her. "I didn't mean to make it seem like I didn't want your help. It's just…the whole thing is weird. I promise I'll let you know what's going on. Right now, there's not much to tell. It's those stupid emails and a weird phone call. If it weren't for the robbery, I probably wouldn't think of it at all. I've been so on edge ever since that happened." Marley fiddled with her fork absently.

Lacey set her pizza down and grabbed Marley's hand. "Of course you're on edge! It would be weird if you weren't. And don't think I'm mad. I'm just worried. If you ask me though, Gage must like you a whole lot. Guys don't just do things like that unless they really care. When can I stop by and meet him?" she asked slyly.

Marley's heart lifted. She took a bite of

pizza before responding. "How about you stop by the lodge tonight? Delia's having another one of her local's dinners. I was thinking of going."

* * *

GAGE STOOD at the doorway that led from the kitchen into the restaurant. He couldn't quite believe what Delia had done, but it was amazing. Christmas was two weeks away, and her local's nights were a rousing success. His hazy childhood memories of a busy restaurant and delicious food couldn't compete with the reality of now. The lodge restaurant was packed. Marley had told him she'd be here for dinner tonight, and he was strangely nervous. Though they'd been spending every night together, she usually worked until he showed up at her place or vice versa. He wanted her to see how well things were progressing at the lodge and felt a thrill of pride when he thought about it.

Aidan had few updates for him the last few days, which irked Gage. He wanted movement on the investigation. He was reconsidering whether he'd head to Seattle next week to see if he could jumpstart things around Kent. According to Aidan, ever since Kent made the call to Marley, his emails and other online activity had gone quiet. The only thing holding Gage back was that he didn't want to leave Marley's side. The way he felt about her was starting to make him uncomfortable—not because he wanted it to go away, but because he'd never experienced anything like it. He was used to being in control in all situations. He'd considered himself immune to this kind of thing. He'd watched a few of his fellow Navy SEALs get tossed around in the storm of relationships and considered it a weakness.

Now, he realized he'd had absolutely no clue what they'd been going through. Marley had breezed her way into his heart, body and soul, and he couldn't imagine how to manage how he felt. Every so often, the word *love* traveled through his brain and he swatted it away. Love meant commitment. Commitment was something he understood very well since he'd committed his life to the SEAL's for years. But the kind of emotional commitment involved in relationships was something he'd purposefully steered away from because it conflicted with the commitment to his career before. With that part of his life in the rear view mirror, he felt unsteady and uncertain about how to handle the feelings Marley elicited. They were entirely beyond his experience and bumped against his desire to plan and stay in control. He didn't know how she fit inside his life. And yet, he couldn't imagine life without Marley. The idea of her not being a part of his life, even worse being with someone else, nearly unhinged him. His carefully controlled and planned life hadn't prepared him for her.

His sisters, Jessa and Becca, would be up tomorrow. Which had him thinking a lot about Marley and how to introduce her to them. He'd never introduced any woman to his family. Jessa and Becca would be the warm up for the rest of his family who were arriving on staggered dates leading up to Christmas. He didn't think of himself as sentimental, but as the reality of Last Frontier Lodge firmed in front of his eyes, he'd become determined his family would be here for the holiday as they used to do for so many years before the lodge closed. Gage was pulled out of his thoughts by a loud crash in the kitchen.

He turned and saw one of the kitchen staff had dropped a large glass jar of olives on the floor. Broken glass and olives dotted the floor. Delia was shaking her head and laughing. "It wouldn't be right if something didn't break on our first full night." She stepped over to help, but Gage beat her to it.

"I got this," he said, waving her away. "You've got food to serve."

The young woman who'd dropped the jar was flushed red. 'I'm so sorry…"

Gage glanced up and shook his head. "You heard Delia, nothing to worry about. Go do what you need to do, and I'll get this." She nodded with alacrity and turned away.

After he swept up the mess and mopped the area, Gage raced upstairs to change when he noticed he still wore the clothes he'd had on when he helped Don outside. When he returned to the restaurant, he saw Marley walking in with a woman who had to be related to her. She shared Marley's hair though it had less red to it. He made his way across the room to Marley's side.

"Hey, there," he said.

Marley glanced up, her forest green eyes landing on his, and his pulse quickened. She affected him as no one ever had. All she had to do was be there, and it was as if she flicked a switch. He talked his body down. The last thing he wanted was to meet anyone related to Marley with an obvious hard on.

The woman at Marley's side glanced up, her eyes similar to Marley's. She held her hand out. When he took it, her grip was firm, her handshake confident. "I'm Lacey, Marley's little sister," she offered brightly. Her eyes held his in an assessing look.

"I'm Gage, I'm, uh..." He realized he'd just been wondering how to introduce Marley to his family and he didn't know how Marley wanted him known to hers.

Lacey interjected. "Boyfriend?" she asked, her tone helpful.

Gage glanced to Marley who nodded.

"That would be me," Gage said with more confidence than he felt. He was on such foreign terrain with his feelings for Marley, he felt adrift. But he didn't want to be anywhere other than right by her side, so he was partially relieved to have Lacey label him.

Lacey smiled widely. "It's great to meet you. Marley's told me all about you and what you've been doing here at the lodge.

You have no idea how excited I am that Last Frontier Lodge will be up and running again! It's my favorite place to ski."

Marley grinned at Lacey and turned to him. "Like I told you, Lacey and I used to ski here all the time when we were kids. She's hardcore though, so you'd better make sure Don gets the advanced trails ready."

Conversation moved on as Marley shared what Lacey did as a guide, pride evident in her tone. Lacey wandered off to greet some friends when it occurred to Gage they'd better grab a table. He spied an open one and took Marley's hand, leading her over to it. "Is your mother here again?" he asked as they sat down.

Marley glanced around the room. "She's not here yet, but I bet she'll be here. She's been coming every time Delia hosts these. Now that Delia's done this, I think she's going to have to keep it up even after you're running at full speed. People are hooked on the idea that you have special prices for locals only."

"I suggested the same thing to her this morning. She did it to get the staff ready for running when the restaurant was busy, but it's been great." He paused to look around again. The room had a hum of conversation and staff bustled among the tables, taking orders, serving drinks and more. This was the second evening when Delia had the bar fully stocked and staffed. They'd had to wait for the liquor license to be approved. Gage had quickly discovered a liquor license was worth far more than its weight in gold. The one night they'd been able to serve from the bar had brought in the first day of profit for the lodge.

When his gaze made its way back to Marley, his heart tightened. Her auburn curls fell loosely around her shoulders, the lights catching in her hair. Her green eyes were bright. She fiddled with a silver chain around her neck. She met his eyes and smiled. "Have you checked the reservations today?"

He shook his head, and she rolled her eyes. "Seriously, Gage? I showed you how to do it. You're perfectly capable of doing it yourself."

He shrugged sheepishly. "Maybe so, but I'd rather have you do it." His answer was entirely true, but he also wanted any reason to keep Marley involved in the lodge. Aside from the logistical help she'd provided, he appreciated her opinion and didn't want her to back off from her involvement. And he just plain wanted her around.

"At some point, you'll have to figure it out."

"That's what I'm paying you to do," he countered.

Marley shook her head. "Fair enough."

She started to say something else when Lacey pulled the chair out beside Marley and sat down with a sigh. Lacey glanced between Marley and Gage. "Am I interrupting a romantic interlude?" she asked with a sly grin.

Marley flushed, and Gage felt his heart clench again. He didn't mind Lacey joining them for dinner, in fact he welcomed it because a chance to get to know anyone close to Marley was a good thing, but any moment he didn't have alone with Marley was a missed opportunity. *Man, you have it bad. As if I didn't know.*

Gage met Lacey's eyes. "Even if you were, I hope you're planning to join us for dinner."

Lacey's grin widened. "Oh, you're good."

Their conversation paused when a waitress arrived to take their orders. As soon as she stepped away, Lacey turned back to him, her expression serious. "Marley told me how you're helping out with the investigation. I wanted to thank you. She hates asking for help, so I can't tell you how relieved I am to know that you're stepping up anyway."

Gage nodded and shifted his shoulders. He glanced to Marley. Her cheeks were bright, and she fiddled with the silverware. He sensed her discomfort and the vulnerability she tried so hard to hide. He glanced back to Lacey. "Glad to help."

Lacey held his gaze for a moment, her eyes bouncing to Marley and back again. She appeared to be considering her words. "Would you mind letting me know when you have any updates?"

Marley's head whipped up. "Lacey..." her tone held an edge of exasperation.

Lacey shrugged. "I'm asking him because I know you. You won't say anything until way after the fact. You're my sister, and I want to make sure you're okay. If Gage will keep me up to date, then you don't have to worry about it."

Marley bit her lip and sighed. "Fine." She glanced up at Gage. "She's cranky because I only just mentioned the emails to her today."

Gage wasn't certain what the correct answer was here, so he opted for nodding. Lacey grinned and let the topic go, moving on to quiz Gage on his entire life story. He found himself oddly pleased at her many questions, as she unabashedly made it clear she was making sure he was good enough for Marley. He'd have expected this to make him uncomfortable, but it didn't. He only hoped he was good enough for Marley because whether he knew how to deal with his feelings or not, he damn sure couldn't fathom stepping aside. As Lacey's quiz continued, he had to do his usual dodge and offer vague answers about his work as a SEAL.

Lacey hitched a brow up. "Are you being vague because you can't tell me, or are you being annoying?" she asked archly.

Marley giggled and shook her head. "I should have warned you Lacey can be pushy."

Gage chuckled. "No problem. I'm being vague because Navy SEAL assignments are almost always classified. Force of habit."

Marley tilted her head, her green eyes

slanting to him. "I'm usually not as nosy as Lacey, but now that she's on a roll, how long ago did you retire from the military?"

Gage's chest tightened slightly. "Just last year. I hadn't been on any assignments for a while and had been doing administrative stuff on base. It wasn't the best fit for me, and I was ready to retire, so I did. Not much later, Gram passed away and I knew where I needed to go." He glossed over the details with such broad strokes it made the situation sound simple. In reality, he'd been tossed asunder by Matt's death. He'd gritted through it on the assignment, but Matt had been his best friend since high school. They'd enlisted in the Navy together after college. Matt had shared every step of his journey on the way to becoming a Navy SEAL. That kind of work deepened bonds for all of the team members, but the bond between him and Matt had begun long before that. Even now, Gage felt a lingering guilt that Matt had been the one to die rather than him. Matt had a wife and child while Gage had no one...until now.

He met Marley's eyes, and his heart clenched painfully. If he had died, he would have missed the chance to meet Marley.

Now that she'd waltzed her way effortlessly into his life and heart, the thought that he could have missed the chance to be with her made his stomach feel hollow. He didn't know what it meant, but if he could do anything to honor Matt's memory, it would be to be as good to the people he loved as Matt had been. *Love*. The word he'd been avoiding. He slipped his hand across Marley's shoulders and laced his fingers in her hair. Without a thought of where they were, he captured her luscious lips in a kiss. In seconds, lust was pounding through him.

Lacey's voice broke into the moment. "Well, hot damn! Geez, I'm not sure what I said to make that happen."

Gage pulled away, his eyes snagging on Marley's. Sweet electricity sizzled in her gaze. With a shake of her head, she broke away and looked around. Gage turned to Lacey and shrugged. "Sorry. Got a little carried away there."

Lacey grinned. "You just made my day. Marley's the best sister in the world, and she deserves an awesome guy. For the moment, you're passing the test."

Gage chuckled and glanced at Marley. She was flushed, her lips swollen from his kiss. He was thankful for the table, as his cock had some pretty strong and hard opinions about what he should be doing with Marley right about now. He took a breath, his pulse racing when she turned his way again and smiled softly.

CHAPTER 16

*M*arley walked downstairs in her cabin and paused to look out the front windows. Snow had fallen during the night, blanketing the field in fluffy white. A pair of moose stood at the edge of the field, nibbling on alders. Their breath billowed in mist around them. Snow sparkled where the sun struck it, glistening under its warmth. A stellar jay squawked and burst out of the trees, landing with such force on a bird feeder by the deck railing that the feeder swung wildly. The sky was clear, and the wind stirred the surface of the bay. The mountains across stood quiet and majestic, their peaks stark white against the bright blue sky.

Marley took a last look and stepped to the kitchen for a cup of coffee. Gage had made a pot of coffee earlier before he left for the lodge. She'd been pleased to discover they both liked their coffee rich and dark. She enjoyed a sip as she considered last night. Watching Gage interact with Lacey had been amusing…and disconcerting. He seemed more than ready to make it clear they were a couple. His hands had been all over her during dinner, pushing the edge of what was socially appropriate in the middle of a restaurant. The moment they'd walked through the door into her cabin, he'd proceeded to drive her wild, bringing her to the delicious edge of sanity—as he did on an almost nightly basis now.

Problem was, she was starting to feel like she was in over her head. Way over her head. Her head had taken a backseat to her heart and body, and she couldn't seem to think clearly. Watching Lacey quiz Gage last night had been enlightening. She'd learned a bit more about him than she'd known herself. Not because she hadn't been curious, but because she tended to be reserved herself, so she rarely pumped people for information about themselves. Lacey had no such compunctions and asked Gage question upon question. Marley sensed there were a few details she was missing when it came to his time as a Navy SEAL. His expression shuttered whenever he spoke of it. There was a thread of pain somewhere in there. Given how much he was coming to mean to her, Marley couldn't help but wonder.

When she'd come home to pull herself together and regain her footing, it had never crossed her mind she'd meet someone like Gage who would call to her heart, body and soul so deeply. She also never in a million years would have thought a man who looked like him would be interested in her. He was all hard-bodied perfection with a smile to die for, and those silvery-gray eyes could make any woman melt on the spot. And yet, when he looked at her, it was as if she was the only woman in the world and he'd been starving for the sight of her.

She took another sip of her coffee, savoring the bracing bite to it. She forced her thoughts off of Gage and sat down at her desk to get to work. She dove into her work, adding some new photos to the blog on the lodge website and then focusing on her latest app project, which was close to completion. It was early afternoon when her email pinged again, and unease snaked up her spine. There were two emails from the alleged human resources account, the first reiterating prior requests that she return the flash drive that she didn't have and the second demanding a call to human resources by a certain date, which happened to be a week before Christmas. Knowing what she knew now, that these emails were being sent by Kent, her unease was joined by anger. She didn't know what his game was and what he wanted, but she was tired of it.

She pushed away from her desk. After stepping into her boots and throwing her jacket on, she headed to the lodge. She didn't plan to sit on this anymore.

* * *

GAGE STOOD at the top of the most advanced ski trail and slowly turned in a circle. The top of this peak was by no means the tallest peak in the area, however the ranges north of Diamond Creek and across Kachemak Bay were distant enough that the vantage point here offered a three hundred and sixty degree view of the area. He took a deep breath, the chilled air energizing him. The mountains rose tall, their snow-covered peaks stark against the sky. Clusters of evergreens stood out against the snow blanketing the landscape. Winter was here to stay with last night's snowfall adding more than a foot of snow to what had already fallen.

The sun was already beginning its slide down the sky even though it was early afternoon. Winter days were short in Diamond Creek. Evenings were a long, slow dance with dusk. Gage had ridden up here with Don on a snowmobile he'd found in the garage a while back. Gage had spent a morning fiddling with the engine and getting it back in running shape. They'd just finished installing the last of the new ski lifts. Don had spent the morning putting Gage through the paces of operating and troubleshooting them. With Don's help, Gage felt like he was getting a handle on the nuts and bolts of running a ski lodge. Delia had worked wonders with the kitchen, reception and housekeeping staff. Opening day was a mere two weeks away now, and he thought they might be able to pull it off.

He glanced at his watch and turned to check on Don who'd stepped into the small hut by the ski lift. These existed at every stopping point on the trails and had emergency medical equipment and warming supplies if needed. Each building was equipped with a woodstove, a bench, a small supply closet with tools for potential lift repairs, and a cabinet of medical supplies.

"Hey Don, you about ready to head down?"

Don glanced up from the cabinet open in front of him. "Yup. Finished stocking this one." He closed the cabinet and zipped a small duffel bag on the bench before slinging it over his shoulder.

"What time do you need to leave to pick up your sisters?" Don asked as they walked over to the snowmobile.

"About an hour," Gage replied.

At Don's nod, Gage climbed on the front of the snowmobile with Don seated behind him. They zipped down the slope, arriving at the lodge within minutes. After he parked the snowmobile in the garage and Don headed off, Gage walked onto the back deck of the lodge. The three main trails converged at the bottom. Higher up the mountain, the trails bisected further with the more advanced trails marching further up the mountainside. As Gage looked up the trails, a small form stepped out from the trees. He knew instantly it was Marley. Her cabin was a short hike through the woods. Her auburn hair swirled in the breeze. Her arms swung loosely at her sides as she strode toward the deck.

His body tightened at the sight of her. He'd given up thinking he could control himself when it came to Marley. All he had to do was think about her, and lust surged through his veins. When she got close enough for him to see her expression, he forgot his pulse of desire. Her eyes held a glimmer of fear and anger, her mouth was in a tight line.

He stepped across the deck to meet her. "What's going on?"

She stopped immediately in front of him, her breath coming out in a rush. "He sent two more emails! Now he wants me to call by next week. Can we call your friend? I'm tired of waiting." Her words tumbled out rapidly. The wind blew a curl across her eyes, and she impatiently brushed it out of the way.

He heard her words, but couldn't think past the anger flashing through him. Whatever this Kent guy was up to, Gage was infuriated with the game he was playing with Marley. He couldn't stand seeing the fear she tried so hard to hide. He clenched and unclenched his fist.

Marley reached out and placed her hand on his arm. His muscles were coiled tight under her touch. "Gage?"

He brought his focus back to the moment. As much as he wanted Kent to be standing in front of him, so he could beat him senseless, Kent was nowhere near and would never be anywhere near Marley if Gage had anything to say about it. Gage took a slow breath and met Marley's eyes. "Yeah?"

"Did you hear me?"

He nodded, reeling his anger further in. "Oh yeah. I heard you. Just thinking for a minute." He slipped his hand in her elbow. "Let's go call Aidan now."

As soon as the door shut on his private apartment upstairs, Gage tugged his phone out and called Aidan.

"Aidan, here."

"You keep telling me we need to bide our time, but I'm done. Kent sent two more emails today, and we need to put a stop to it."

Marley turned from where she'd walked to the windows, her eyes wide. Gage was tired of being patient and didn't give a damn if it meant Marley sensed his frustration.

Aidan was silent for a moment. "I planned to call this afternoon anyway because those emails blipped on our radar too. Before you get ahead of yourself, can you trust me to follow up with the police and not fly down here and knock his lights out?"

Gage had worked with Aidan for most of his time in the military. He'd never lost his cool and could easily shrug off Aidan's propensity for sarcasm. Not now. The voice of reason was drowned out by his worry for Marley. "Fuck off, dude. I'm pissed and I want some movement on this. I've got enough sense to let you do what you do, but if someone doesn't put a stop to this bullshit by the end of the week, I will come down there."

Aidan chuckled. "Right. Already have a

call in to the lead detective. I'm meeting with him later this week."

Gage took another breath. "Fine. Look, uh, I don't mean to sound like an asshole…"

"No worries. Can't wait to meet Marley though because I never thought I'd see you like this over a woman."

Gage couldn't hold back the laugh that barked out. "Fair enough. How about you fly up for a week of skiing sometime soon? You can meet Marley then. But only after this thing is dealt with."

"I'd love to. Meantime, gotta go. I'll call you after my meeting."

The line went dead before Gage had a chance to reply. He tucked the phone in his pocket and turned to Marley. She stood by the windows, her back to him and her arms wrapped around her waist. He walked toward her, rolling his neck around to ease the tension knotted there. He came to stand behind her, resting his hands on her hunched shoulders. Hot anger simmered inside. The only thing keeping Gage from showing up at Kent's door was the fact that he happened to be a long plane ride away, and Gage didn't want to leave Marley alone right now.

"Well?" she asked.

Gage marshaled his composure. He didn't want to contemplate Aidan's point, but it was accurate that Gage had never had a woman affect him like this. Hell, nothing and no one affected him like this. Even when his best friend died, he'd stayed cool and calm, battening his emotions down behind his well-honed walls of discipline and will. He smoothed his hands along Marley's shoulders and down her arms, willing her to relax. She smelled like vanilla and honey with a bite of cold winter air clinging to her.

"Aidan tracked the emails already. He has a meeting with the lead detective later this week. He'll call me after that."

Marley nodded. "Okay."

Gage slid his palms around her waist, savoring the soft curve of her belly under his hands, and held her close. The tension in her shoulders eased slightly. He nuzzled her hair out of the way and rested his chin on her shoulder. His heart clenched, almost to the point of pain. *This*...this intense protectiveness was foreign to him. He'd spent his military career committed to the protection of others and didn't bat an eye at the weight of that responsibility. He and his team had put their lives on the line time and again. Yet, none of those experiences had prepared him for what it felt like to have someone matter as much as Marley mattered to him. At this moment, her life wasn't in danger, not that he knew. She was dealing with annoying emails on the heels of an assault and robbery. Nothing came close to some of the situations he'd faced before—and nothing came close to the way he felt about her.

Marley turned in his arms. When her forest green eyes met his, he almost lost his breath. The coil of anger inside morphed into an intense want. He lifted a hand to tuck a loose lock of hair behind her ear, and a tremor ran through it. Her cheeks were still red from the cold outside, the scattering of freckles on her skin stood out. He leaned to kiss her when his phone buzzed in his pocket.

"Ignore it."

"Don't you have to pick up your sisters?"

"Dammit, yes." He tugged his phone out and saw Jessa's name blinking on the screen.

"Hey," he answered, more sharply than he intended.

"Hey Gage!"

"Hey Jessa, what time are you due at the airport?"

"We're changing planes in Anchorage. We're supposed to make it to Homer in an hour. Just checking to make sure you'll be there to pick us up."

"Of course. See you in a bit." He ended the call quickly. Jessa was prone to chatter about anything and everything if given the time.

Gage met Marley's eyes again. "That was Jessa." He glanced at his watch. "I'll need to leave in a bit here. Want to go with me?"

He hadn't planned to take Marley with him, but it suddenly seemed like the best plan. He wouldn't have to leave her side, and it might be the ideal way for his sisters to meet her. He'd be able to blow through the whole introduction thing.

Marley's expression was puzzled. "You want me to go with you?"

He nodded firmly. "Yes. You can meet Becca and Jessa. They'll be thrilled."

"I don't want to interrupt your time with them..."

"You won't be interrupting."

Gage couldn't say that he suddenly couldn't bear to leave her alone. He didn't know how to manage the depth of feelings for her. *Man, you are in too deep. You're freaking out over a few emails.* Gage gritted his teeth, annoyed with his own mind. *It's not just a few emails. She got robbed and assaulted. Months ago, man. That was months ago. You know better than to assume these emails have something to do with that.* He shook his head, shutting down the internal debate. Problem was, he did know better than to instantly draw connections, but he also trusted his gut. His gut told him these emails had something to do with that robbery.

"Gage?"

He glanced down into those green, green eyes of Marley's that seemed to have the power to cast a spell over him. He'd been quiet longer than he'd been aware. "Sorry. Just thinking. How about we pick them up and grab dinner together on the way back?"

Marley finally nodded, and his breath released. She stepped back. "We should go then. We have just enough time to get there."

CHAPTER 17

Marley watched the landscape roll by as Gage drove south to Homer. The mountains were bright—alpenglow reflecting in soft rose and lavender against the snow as the sun dropped down the sky. They'd passed a few moose on the drive, along with a porcupine who'd carefully made its way through the snow to deftly climb up a spruce tree as it watched them drive by. Marley was hyper aware of Gage's presence. She kept waiting for the charge that buzzed between them to start to fade, and yet it kept sizzling higher. She was flushed inside and out simply sitting beside him in the car.

He'd startled her when he'd asked her to

go with him to pick up his sisters. The idea of meeting his family seemed so…official. He didn't speak of them often, but when he did, he spoke with warmth. His tendency toward reserve only offered flashes of his feelings. He'd now met both of her parents and Lacey at different times when they'd gone to the lodge restaurant for dinners, but somehow that seemed less meaningful. Her family was such a part of her daily life in Diamond Creek, it would have been strange if Gage hadn't met them yet.

She glanced sideways. She could look at the angled planes of his face all day. His face bore the strength of the rest of him. His sensuous lips sent her pulse skittering. He slanted his eyes to her—a flash of gray lightning landed on her before his lips quirked and he looked back at the road. His palm rested on her thigh, warm through the denim of her jeans. He gave a subtle squeeze, tightening the coil of desire inside. Her belly fluttered, and she shifted restlessly. He began to stroke up and down her leg, dipping into the soft curve behind her knee, his thumb stroking between her thighs. Her breath ran away from her— short, soft gasps that she tried to quiet.

Gage kept driving, one hand on the wheel, his eyes firmly on the road, and his free hand driving her to distraction. Hot, liquid need swirled through her. His thumb kept teasing her, right at the center of her desire. Rough touches through the denim and then moving away, almost bringing her to madness. Heat twisted inside.

"Gage..." she whispered fiercely. "You're driving, you can't..." Her voice broke on a gasp when he cupped her mound. She was so wet, it wouldn't have surprised her if he could feel it through her jeans. He suddenly slowed the car as they approached an un-marked gravel road. He swung abruptly onto the road, gunning his truck briefly and turning into an empty clearing that ap-peared to be a trailhead of sorts though snow blanketed the small parking area.

The truck stopped with a jerk. Gage turned to her, his smoky gaze tracking over her, burning her with its intensity. The space yawned between them though he was so close, no more than a foot separating them. His motions deliberate, he adjusted the truck's bench seat, sliding it all the way back, his eyes glued to her. Marley could barely breathe. Her heart was beating so hard, she could hear it. With a squeeze that pushed her to the delicious edge of pleasure, he dragged his hand up. Her jacket hung open. He shoved it out of the way and roughly tore at her blouse, swearing when a button caught. His hand curled around the back of her neck as he leaned to meet her. He fit his mouth, open and hot, to hers and seared her with a kiss.

If she hadn't been seated, she'd have collapsed. A wild flame licked inside as she scrambled to get closer. She couldn't get enough…ever. Gage's hands finally managed to open her blouse, the rough skin of his palms coasting up her sides, his thumbs caressing her tight peaked nipples through the silk of her bra. Hampered by the tight space in his truck, Marley became frenzied. Turning toward him, she ran her hands up his abdomen and chest, frantic to feel his skin. He chuckled when she swore, and then swiftly undid the clasp of her bra, curling his hands around her breasts. He rolled her nipples, tight and achy, between his fingers. She tumbled into the cloud of desire that swirled around them. He caught her lower lip between his teeth as he pulled away from her lips. He leaned back for a moment.

"You are so beautiful," he whispered, his eyes fierce as they coasted across her face and down to her breasts, heavy and full in his hands.

She could hardly think. Her core drew tight, liquid heat drenching her. His lips closed over a nipple, and she cried out, arching into his touch, desperate for more. He alternated sucking, stroking and nipping before he pulled away, his smoky gaze searing through her. She pushed him back and tore at the buttons of his jeans, curling her hand around his hard shaft. He murmured her name, his voice low and taut. She freed him from the confines of his jeans, stroking the velvet length of his cock. He captured her lips in a kiss again, his tongue sweeping in deeply, his hand curling around her neck to pull her closer. She tore her lips away and shoved him back against the door, taking him in her mouth. She took him all the way in, the head of his cock bumping against the back of her throat as she swiftly stroked up and down, glorying in the husky groans that tore from him.

Suddenly, he moved, lifting her up and tearing at her jeans. In spite of the cramped space, she somehow got her jeans off. Gage growled his approval when he cupped his hand over her panties and stroked her through the wet silk. Not bothering with those, he shifted and effortlessly lifted her onto his lap. No matter how many times he held her in his arms, she marveled at his raw strength. When her knees fell to either side of his hips and she rested against the heated length of his arousal, he groaned. She shoved her hands under his shirt, pushing it up to feel some of his skin. A ragged breath broke from him when she pressed her hips down on him. Pleasure spiked at the feel of him against her core, dripping with need. He shoved her panties out of the way, dragging his fingers through her folds.

Her forehead fell to his, their breath mingling as he drove his fingers into her. She was so close to the edge, she could hardly stand it. Pressure gathered and gathered as he stroked into her with his fingers. He adjusted his hips when he pulled his fingers away, the tip of his cock resting at her entrance. He held still and whispered her name. She dragged her eyes open to find his waiting. The world had narrowed to this moment and nothing else. In the falling darkness on a deserted snowy road, the rush of intimacy between them flared. Gage held her eyes in his smoky gray gaze as he sheathed himself inside of her. He began to move incrementally, rocking his hips into her. He cupped the back of her head, threading his hand into her hair. Sensation unfurled through her, tremors of pleasure building and building until her climax crashed over her. As she shuddered around him, clenching him in her channel, his head fell back, her name coming out in a ragged cry as he pulsed into her.

Her head dropped into the curve of his neck as she tried to catch her breath. His hand loosened in her curls and slid down her spine. Only when she heard the bump of his hand on the steering wheel did she remember where they were. His hand stroked in slow circles on her back. She eventually lifted her head and looked around. Gage had left the truck running and heat blew across them. It was almost dark outside, the snow bright in the gloaming. Marley turned to Gage. He rolled his head to the side, his mouth curling at one corner.

Her chest tightened. Emotion washed over her, the intimacy between them so deep, she didn't know how to comprehend it. He held her eyes and reached a hand up to tuck a curl behind her ears.

"I think we might be late." His words were gruff.

Marley felt a warm swell inside and giggled. "We're definitely late."

Gage met hers eyes, his smile all she wanted. "Right. I suppose we should get going."

They slowly untangled themselves and put themselves back together. When Gage stopped before turning back on the highway, Marley pulled the visor down and glanced at herself in the mirror. "Oh no. My hair's a mess," she commented and started running her fingers through it, a feeble attempt to tidy it.

He put his hand on her thigh and squeezed. "You look beautiful. Stop worrying."

She turned to him, about to argue, and then saw the look in his eyes. He held her in his gaze—desire and something else in its depths.

"Okay," she said softly. She leaned back in the seat and curled her hand over his.

Not much later, he crested the hill where the highway rose up before dipping down into Homer. The lights of the town glittered ahead. Homer sat at the end of the road, literally. The highway ended at the end of the Homer Spit, the longest 'spit' in the world. A spit was a small, narrow peninsula of land. The Homer Spit was four and a half miles long and was the longest road into ocean waters in the world. Marley had always loved visiting the spit. It felt like driving on a land bridge into the ocean. Homer's airport was the closest sizable airport to Diamond Creek, a mere hour away. Diamond Creek had what was referred to as a 'puddle jumper' airport, primarily serving small planes that flew in rural areas of Alaska. Homer had an airport that could accommodate full-size commercial airliners, so it was the common destination for people coming to Diamond Creek from out of state.

When Gage drove down the hill into town, Marley directed him to the airport. As they drove through the small town, she glanced over at him. "We should visit here in the daytime."

He nodded and squeezed her leg. "I've heard it's a great place to fish. Do they have a ski lodge here?"

She giggled, realizing he was sizing up

potential competition. "Nope, no ski lodge. Lots of art galleries, shopping and fishing. We can come in the summer."

As the words left her mouth, she realized she was unconsciously assuming they'd be together next summer. Gage's quick affirmative reply startled her and curled around her heart. Thrumming in the aftermath of their earlier encounter, her anxiety at meeting his sisters was forgotten.

Moments later, he pulled up at the airport. They walked inside, a blast of heat hitting them when they walked through the automatic doors. Marley's eyes were adjusting to the light when there was a squeal. She turned to find Gage surrounded by two women, both hugging him at once. After the flurry of welcome, Gage stepped back. His gray eyes were bright. Marley knew without a doubt he was happy to see his sisters. One stood tall, close to Gage's height, with glossy straight brown hair that hung halfway down her back. The other was petite and curvy with long chocolate brown hair brightened with blonde streaks. The women turned at once to look at Marley. She felt as if she were under a microscope.

Gage stepped back to Marley's side,

sliding his arm around her waist. "This is Marley. He paused and glanced down at her. "She's my girlfriend. Thought you two might want to meet her."

In unison, both women arched a brow. The only word to describe their shared expression was startled. They looked at Marley and back to Gage. The shorter woman smiled slowly before rushing at Marley and hugging her. "Oh my God! This is the best!" She turned to Gage. "How come you didn't say anything?" Her eyes filled with tears as she stepped back. Her eyes were a softer shade of gray than Gage's, almost silvery. She held a hand out, which seemed silly after her rapturous hug, but Marley reached for her hand and shook it.

"I'm Jessa. I didn't mean to seem crazy, but Gage has never brought anyone to meet us, so you must mean a lot to him. Nice to meet you. You look super nice," she said warmly.

"Uh, okay. Nice to meet you too," Marley replied. Her mind spun to hear she was the first woman Gage had introduced to his family. Her heart leapt at the possible implications of that, a warm flush spiraling through her.

The other sister angled her head to the side, her blue eyes bouncing between them. Her gaze was curious, but certainly not quite as warm as Jessa's. She took a quick stride to Marley and held her hand out. "Becca," she said firmly when Marley shook her hand. "As Jessa mentioned, Gage isn't much for introducing us to anyone. I take it you do mean a lot to him, so you'd better be good to him." She slanted her eyes to Gage. "Gage's tendency to be insanely private isn't particularly helpful."

Anxiety swirled inside Marley. She couldn't help it, but she wanted Gage's sisters to like her. Becca was intimidating to say the least. She met Becca's eyes and tried to smile. Gage's arm tightened around her waist. "Ease up, Becca." He glanced down at Marley. "Becca's kind of a badass. She's a public prosecutor and spends so much time facing the seedy side of the world, she isn't the most optimistic person. But she has a heart of gold, she just doesn't let everyone see it."

Marley nodded. Becca's eyes softened, and she cuffed Gage on the shoulder. She glanced back to Marley. "Gage means a lot to us. I can be kind of protective."

Marley nodded again, feeling silly at this point. Jessa grinned and clasped her hands together. "This is so perfect! You came back to Alaska and fell in love."

Gage chuckled. Marley couldn't help but notice he didn't bother to correct Jessa. Conversation moved on to getting their bags. After a flurry of activity, they were piled in Gage's truck. Marley insisted on riding in one of the small seats in the back with Jessa because Becca's tall form would be cramped in the tiny space. Though Gage had started to argue the point, Marley ignored him.

"It's about damn time is all I have to say!" Jessa declared with a lift of her wine glass before she downed its remainder.

Becca grinned and shook her head. "Good thing you don't have to drive anywhere tonight," she commented wryly. "You are such a lightweight."

Jessa shrugged and turned her smile on Marley. "I mean it. I pretty much gave up on Gage ever getting involved with anyone. It's obvious he adores you. So there," she said firmly.

They were seated at a corner booth in the lodge restaurant. It was late afternoon, so the restaurant wasn't filled at the moment. Business had been so good, Delia had begun to keep the restaurant open for dinners every night. Gage was busy helping Don repair the snowmobile, which had gotten cranky this afternoon and refused to start. Given that opening day was quite close, they needed the snowmobile for quick travel on the slopes. Gage and Don shared the tendency to want to fix anything and everything, so he'd dropped a quick kiss on Marley's cheek and promised her he'd be up to meet them for dinner once he and Don were done.

Jessa and Becca had settled in at the lodge and quickly made themselves helpful in the few days they'd been there. Marley felt a lingering self-consciousness with Becca who remained reserved though she appeared to be reserved with most everyone, so at least Marley wasn't getting special treatment. Jessa, on the other hand, was a font of warmth. When Jessa came across Marley in the hall on her way out, she'd tucked her hand in Marley's elbow and dragged her into an early happy hour with Becca.

Marley met Jessa's silver gaze and couldn't hide her blush. "Well, I wouldn't know if he adored me, but he's pretty awesome."

Jessa nodded emphatically and refilled their wineglasses. She turned to Becca. "Why are you so uptight about this?"

Becca's expression was difficult to read. Marley sensed Becca was uncomfortable with Gage's relationship with her, and she wanted to know why. Becca glanced between Jessa and Marley before she sighed. "I don't mean to come across like that." She turned to Marley, her gaze softening. "Gage is a really good guy, but he's never been interested in relationships. Part of that was because of his time in the military, but I also thought it was because it didn't come easy to him. He's been through a lot the last few years. It's big that he's seeing anyone. He's always been the one to be strong for anyone who needed him. I'm happy he's found someone, but I'm pretty protective of him. I don't want to see him get hurt. So if I seem uptight, it's just because I'm not sure what he means to you. For what it's worth, I don't know what he's said to you, but there isn't a doubt in my mind that he loves you."

Becca's words hit Marley right in the heart, almost taking her breath away. Her mind spun. The idea that Gage might love her blew open the door she'd been barely holding closed in front of her heart. The idea of love danced at the edges of her thoughts whenever Gage passed through her mind, which was most of the time. But she hadn't dared to allow herself to ponder it much. Because she still hadn't wrapped her brain around the fact that she was falling hard and fast for Gage, she was perpetually trying to scramble for purchase so she could think things through. She felt so out of her depth with Gage. To hear Becca bluntly state that she believed Gage loved her brought hot tears to her eyes.

Marley took a gulp of air, finally looking up to meet Becca's eyes. Becca seemed to see something there. She took a slow breath and nodded thoughtfully. "Well then, I guess I don't need to worry about Gage."

Jessa bumped her shoulder against Becca. "I told you she loved him. I could tell when we were at the airport." Jessa grinned at Marley. "I did tell her, but Becca's not very romantic. She told me I was being ridiculous."

Becca rolled her eyes. She held Marley's

gaze, her eyes assessing. "I'm guessing Gage hasn't mentioned he loves you?"

Marley shook her head, her heart pounding and her throat tight. She was fraught with hope and overwhelmed with her feelings. Questions tumbled through her mind, wondering what Becca meant when she said Gage had been through a lot.

Becca tilted her head. "He's not the most expressive guy around. Give him time."

Marley somehow regained the ability to speak. "What do you mean when you say Gage has been through a lot?"

Becca eyed her and even Jessa's expression sobered. After a long silence, Becca spoke. "His best friend died while they were on a mission in Iraq. He barely talks about it. He can't really because pretty much everything he did as a Navy SEAL was classified, but Matt's death hit him hard."

Jessa reached across the table and grabbed one of Marley's hands, squeezing it in hers. "Gage might be the strong, silent type, but he cares a lot. He's always been there for all of us. After Matt died, he got even more serious. He used to date here and there, but as far as we knew, he hasn't dated anyone for the last few years. I didn't see a spark in him until he started talking about moving up here after Gram died. He hadn't known she still owned the lodge." Jessa released Marley's hand and glanced at Becca. "That's why Becca's been worried about him. I know you don't know us that well, but it's obvious to me he means a lot to you. I'm so happy he found you," she said softly.

Marley's throat tightened again. To consider what it must have been like for Gage to lose his best friend like that tore at her. As his sisters said, he wasn't the most expressive guy. While Marley may have had her uncertainties about how he felt about her, she didn't doubt he cared deeply about those who mattered to him. She cleared her throat. "I appreciate you letting me know a little about him. It helps me understand him," she said softly. She turned to Becca. "I can promise you he means a lot to me. This whole thing with him kind of took me off guard, and I'm not so good at the relationship thing..."

Marley paused when Ginger arrived at their table. She bluntly interrupted Marley. "You mean you haven't dated in almost a decade."

Marley flushed and glared at Ginger.

"We were having a serious conversation." Marley turned to Becca and Jessa and gestured to Ginger. "This is my friend, Ginger. She's kind of nosy."

Ginger pulled her jacket off and sat down beside Marley, giving her a side hug. After a few moments of greetings and ordering food, Ginger zoomed back to the conversation she'd interrupted. "So, what this about you not being good at relationships? You seem to be doing just fine with Gage."

Marley flushed while Jessa grinned. "We were just telling Marley how happy we are about her and Gage."

Ginger glanced between them. "Join the club. I keep telling Marley to relax and accept the fact that Gage totally has the hots for her."

Marley's face was so hot, she thought she might melt. Right then, Gage walked into the restaurant from the kitchen. He slowly made his way across the room. His jeans hung low on his hips, his fitted cotton shirt lifting to reveal a flash of his rock-hard abs when he paused to straighten a chair at an empty table. He caught her eyes when he got closer to their table. Heat swirled in her center, butterflies massing in her belly. She couldn't have looked away from his smoky gray gaze if her life depended on it.

"In case you were wondering how they felt about each other. I swear, one of these days they're going to go up in flames in front of everyone," Ginger commented wryly.

Jessa giggled, and even Becca chuckled. Marley fought her blush, but she knew it was hopeless. As Gage reached the table, Ginger quickly stood and grabbed a chair from a nearby table. She gestured for Gage to take her now empty seat beside Marley. Gage grinned at her and slid into the booth beside Marley. Ginger tugged her chair to the end of the booth.

Gage stretched his arm across the back of the booth, his hand resting at the base of Marley's neck. A shiver ran through her at the subtle touch. She glanced up at Gage. "How'd the repairs go?"

Gage glanced down, his eyes banked with heat, his thumb lightly caressing her neck. "We got it running again. I'll be buying another snowmobile though. We could use more than one around here. This one's hanging in there, but it's probably thirty years old."

Conversation moved on with Ginger peppering Gage with questions about the lodge. At one point, Becca nodded approvingly at Gage. "Gotta say, Gage. I wasn't so sure how you'd manage to get this place up and running this year, but you've pulled it off."

Gage simply nodded, an excellent example of his tendency to be reserved. Marley knew this had been an old childhood dream, and he was on the cusp of making it come true. All he offered was a nod. Marley pondered the glimpse of Gage she'd learned from his sisters and rolled the word *love* around in her mind like a pebble in hand. Her feelings for him frightened her, mostly because he'd come to mean so much, so quickly. Her heart was all in, and her body was a magnet when it came to him. All he had to do was be near, and she spun to him, unable to hold back. To hear Becca state so bluntly that it was obvious Gage loved her...well, that had blown the hinges off of her heart.

Jessa insisted on a toast. "To my oldest brother: here's to your dream coming true."

She paused and met Marley's eyes. "And to love."

Marley flushed straight through. She didn't dare look at Gage and tried to control her expression, though her pulse ricocheted wildly. Glasses clinked and the hum of conversation carried on around them. Gage's hand squeezed her neck softly, his calloused fingers idly toying with the collar of her shirt. A liquid hot shiver raced through her.

* * *

GAGE LIFTED his glass in reply to Jessa's toast and kept his expression neutral. Jessa had taken every opportunity since she'd arrived to proclaim how perfect Marley was for him. Jessa was the most expressive of all of his siblings—the emotional weathervane in the family. She knew him well enough to know he didn't do so well with blatant expressions of emotion, so he sensed she'd decided it was her job to make sure he realized how amazing Marley was. He hadn't the heart to point out to Jessa she didn't need to do any convincing. Barely a moment passed that he wasn't thinking about Marley. He was relieved at how much he had to do during his waking hours, or he'd likely have driven himself to the edge with Marley dancing in his thoughts at all times. His body functioned on high idle around her, always on the edge of arousal with flat-out lust surging whenever she was close.

For example, right now she sat quietly beside him in the booth. His sisters and Ginger chattered away and the restaurant buzzed around them as it slowly filled with people. For all his body cared, they were in the middle of nowhere by themselves. He couldn't keep his hands from touching her someway, somehow, so he resigned himself to stroke the soft skin at the back of her neck. Her thigh was warm against his. His cock was rock hard and conveniently hidden by the table. He'd have to dredge up the fortitude to will his arousal away before he stood up. The temptation to rub his hand along her thigh was so great, he had to grit his teeth. The only thing stopping him was that he knew if he touched her somewhere his hand couldn't be seen, he'd be unable to resist the urge to tease her. He wasn't opposed to public displays of affection, but he wasn't about to go there with the close audience of his sisters and Marley's best friend.

He dared to glance at Marley and closed his eyes at the sight of the flush on her cheeks and the freckles scattered across her skin. In his mind's eyes, he could see the patterns of freckles randomly strewn on her body and how much he enjoyed mapping her body with his mouth meandering along the path of her freckles. Jessa had declared she believed he was in love with Marley, and he supposed he was. Love was a foreign language for him. It also hadn't had any part in his plans. He thought perhaps he needed to find a way to tell Marley how he felt. He was working up to that.

In the meantime, he was restless because Aidan had no news yet. Impatient, Gage had called him this morning to find out the meeting Aidan had with the lead detective had been rescheduled to this afternoon. Gage had called right before he came to dinner, only to get Aidan's voice mail. Gage's thoughts were interrupted by the arrival of their food. He ate mostly with one hand, reluctant to break the link of his touch with Marley.

A while later, he walked through the trees with Marley to her cabin. Though it was dark, an almost full moon offered a silvery walk through the forest. The snow glowed softly under the moon. When they reached her cabin, Marley quickly got to work starting a fire after they kicked their boots off and hung their jackets. Gage had arranged for Jessa and Becca to stay in the private apartment at the lodge and set aside some rooms for the rest of his family. He'd actually had to turn away a few reservations, but he didn't care. He was bound and determined to have his entire family at Last Frontier Lodge for this Christmas.

Becca had arched a brow when he'd explained he was staying at Marley's, while Jessa had squealed and hugged him. Becca tended to be reserved and skeptical, particularly when it came to relationships. She'd been burned badly by her last relationship when her fiancée had dumped her a mere two days before their wedding. Gage didn't know all of the details, but he knew Becca's skepticism when it came to relationships had grown exponentially after that. He had his own tendency to be reserved, so he'd merely shrugged and insisted he'd be staying with Marley.

He turned and looked over at Marley. She was bending over to place a log in the woodstove, her lush bottom tempting him. He started walking toward her when his phone buzzed in his pocket. He almost ignored it when he remembered Aidan should be calling. Slipping his phone out, he glanced at the screen. At the sight of Aidan's name, he answered.

"Hey, what's the update?"

"Hey, nice to talk to you too. I'm doing great, how are you?" Aidan asked sarcastically.

"Fine, fine. Don't mean to be rude, but I figured you're calling for a reason, so let's get to the point."

Aidan chuckled. "Right. The deal is Kent Walker has a problem, namely that he's been having an affair with one of the higher ups at a main competitor of Tech Synergy's. That itself isn't much of a thing, except for the fact that it appears he was leaking project data to her, so they could try to win a few contracts out from under Tech Synergy. Kent doesn't know we know this, but one of my guys tracked down the data Kent thinks Marley has and it's got his fingerprints all over it, including his emails with the woman in question. I'm not sure why he was stupid enough to purposefully save the data that would show the trail, but he did. They broke up, and she went to the police when he tried to blackmail her. Problem is, he lost the flash drive. Why he thinks Marley ever had it, we're not really sure."

Gage swore savagely, and Marley closed the woodstove door and swung around to him, her eyes questioning. Gage took a breath and reined in the fury that welled inside. He held Marley's gaze, mentally warring with himself. He wanted to stay here with her, but he couldn't keep sitting this out. He needed to get to Seattle. He had to see this through. "Okay, I'm coming down tomorrow."

"Figured you'd say that. I'll pick you up at the airport." Aidan started to say something else and then paused.

"What?" Gage asked.

"Well, the detective asked if we thought Marley would be willing to come in for another interview. They're pretty sure Kent was responsible for her robbery, but they're not sure if it was him, or if he had someone else do it. They'd like to question her again to see if she has any details they missed. I'm not sure how you feel about that."

Gage's heart clenched. He glanced to

Marley again who watched him silently. Every fiber of his being wanted to protect her from this, to keep her away from Seattle, a place he knew she'd been relieved to leave. But he knew she wouldn't appreciate his interference. She might decide not to go on her own, but it would be her decision, not his. He forced himself to take a breath. "Let me talk to her about it and let you know. Okay?"

"Of course," Aidan said quickly. "How about you text me your arrival time once you have it?"

"You got it. See you then." Gage ended the call and tossed his phone on the counter nearby.

Marley took a step toward him and stopped. "Who was that?"

"Aidan."

"Oh, um, what did he say?"

Gage found himself fighting to keep his expression in check and his emotions under control. Years of automatic discipline were weak against the depth of protectiveness he felt for Marley. He didn't want to tell her the police wanted to interview her again, didn't want to tell her a man she knew was most likely responsible for her robbery and assault, and desperately didn't want to see any fear flash in her eyes. But he knew this had to be her decision, no matter how much he wanted to shield her from it.

"The police want to interview you again." He forced the words out.

Marley's eyes widened, the fear he hadn't wanted to see flickering. But she lifted her chin and held his gaze. "Why?"

"Because they think Kent is responsible for the robbery and assault, but they're not sure if he did it himself, or if he had someone else do it."

"What?! I don't understand, why…"

Gage quickly summarized what Aidan had shared. Marley leaned against the couch, her arms wrapped around her waist. Gage's throat was tight, his heart knotted with worry. He hated having to tell her any of this. He wanted to go to Seattle, smash Kent's face in and do everything in his power to wipe Marley's memories clean.

He stepped in front of her and curled his hands on her shoulders, slowly pulling her toward him. Her arms fell and she stepped into his embrace. He could feel the tension coiled in her body. He stroked his hands up and down her back, willing her to relax. The heat from the woodstove gradually permeated the cabin. He felt her slowly ease. She finally pulled back and lifted her head. Her gaze speared him right in his heart. In that split second, he knew what he felt was love and he could hardly bear it. Now wasn't the time to say something, so he held his silence, his body thrumming with emotion.

Marley took a slow breath, her expression becoming curious. "It's funny. There were a few rumors at the office about someone maybe passing code onto that company. But there was always talk like that. There were so many start ups, so many projects in development. I can't believe it was actually happening. What was Kent thinking, saving all those emails and data on a flash drive? They're so easy to lose. And why did he think I had it?"

Gage eyed her, relieved she seemed to be okay. "Damned if I know. Aidan said the two things they don't know yet are why Kent thought you might have the flash drive and if he did the robbery himself, or had someone else do it."

Cold fury knotted in Gage's gut every time he thought about what happened to Marley. He remembered Don's description that she'd been pistol whipped before the man tore her apartment to pieces. He closed his eyes and wrestled his emotions under control. Marley didn't need him punching the walls like he wanted to now. He needed to keep it together until he was somewhere he could actually do something.

"I'll go," Marley said abruptly.

"To Seattle?" Gage reminded himself it needed to be her decision, but he was unprepared for how much he didn't want her to go. He wanted her to stay safe here in Diamond Creek.

Marley was unaware of his internal battle when she nodded quickly. "Yup. Will you come with me?"

"Of course! I just told Aidan I was going there myself. I was trying to figure out how to explain it to you. There's no way I'd let you go down there by yourself."

Marley reached up and ran her fingers through his hair. "Good." She paused and tilted her head. "What about Becca and Jessa?"

"They'll understand. We'll go down tomorrow morning and fly back the next morning." He knew his sisters would understand if he explained.

Marley held his eyes for a long moment, her expression soft. "Okay." She stepped out of his arms and walked to her desk. "Let's make reservations now," she said, grabbing her laptop and pulling up a travel website.

Gage rested on the pillows hours later, Marley soft and lush in his arms. He stroked a hand through her hair, marveling at how little control he had when it came to her. He'd climbed in bed tonight, telling himself he could manage one night without the sense-stealing, breathtaking sex that left him gutted at the bare intimacy of it. He was just catching his breath now, his mantra useless against the thread of desire that stitched tighter and tighter between them every day. He glanced down. Her head rested on his shoulders, her auburn hair spread in a tangle. Moonlight cast a beam across the bed, gilding her skin with its silvery light. He closed his eyes and willed himself to sleep, wondering how he was going to keep it together tomorrow. He'd never once questioned his ability to keep his emotions under control in a tense situation. But then, he'd never been in love before.

Marley walked at Gage's side through Pike Place Market. They'd landed in Seattle late this morning and were scheduled to meet with the police this afternoon. She wanted to spend some time with him in one of her favorite places in Seattle, so she'd dragged him here for lunch and a meander through the market. They were heading back toward the hotel now to meet with Aidan. She glanced up at Gage, her heart squeezing with emotion suddenly. They were having a simple, everyday moment, and yet, the joy she felt at being with him came so naturally that it blew her away. His chocolate hair was damp from the soft mist falling. He'd eschewed a raincoat and sauntered at her side, his warm hand laced in hers. She still couldn't quite believe he wanted her. As they walked along, plenty of women gave him a second look, some blatant. She couldn't help the curl of jealousy. She wanted to wave their eyes away and stamp him as hers and hers only. His body was all muscle, his smoky gray gaze sent sparks skittering along her veins with the slightest glance.

He looked down at her, his mouth quirking before he stopped abruptly and turned to her.Without a word, he leaned forward and molded his lips over hers. In the middle of a busy sidewalk with people parting around them, Gage kissed her senseless. He swept his tongue inside her mouth, cupping her cheek with his hand. As swiftly as it began, it ended. He pulled away, his eyes intent on her. His thumb lightly coasted across the pulse beating wildly in her neck. He closed his eyes for a moment. When he opened them again, Marley thought she saw a flash of uncertainty in them.

"Let's get to the hotel," he said gruffly.

Moments later, they walked through the lobby. Marley pulled her raincoat off and gave it a shake while they waited for the elevator. She heard Gage's name and turned toward the voice to see a man walking in their direction. He was tall, dark and solid as a rock. She figured he must be Aidan, who Gage had explained was a former team member from his Navy SEAL days and ran his own private security company now.

Gage grinned and tugged Aidan into a swift hug when he reached them. "Hey man, good to see you." Gage turned and slipped his arm around Marley's waist. "This is Marley."

Aidan's blue eyes crinkled when he smiled at Marley. He held a hand out. "Hello Marley. Nice to meet the woman who's stolen Gage's heart."

Marley shook his hand, which was so large it literally engulfed hers. Though she'd never have considered Gage short by any means, Aidan towered over her and topped Gage. With Gage at roughly six feet, she figured Aidan had to have a good four plus inches on him. Gage chuckled softly at Aidan's comment, while Marley frantically wondered if it was true, or if Aidan was casually teasing.

"Nice to meet you too. I don't know how to thank you…"

Aidan glanced to Gage and back at her. "No need to thank me. Gage is the one who asked me to help, so if you want to thank someone, thank him. I'm happy to help and damn glad we actually got somewhere."

The elevator binged and opened. Aidan gestured for them to go in first. "Let's get somewhere private to talk."

After they got to their hotel room, Marley pushed the curtains back and glanced out over the Seattle skyline. Her old apartment was a few blocks away. She'd been worried about how she'd feel coming back here, but her anxiety was lessened significantly with Gage by her side. The skyline was fuzzy in the misty rain, but she could see the Space Needle in the distance and boats in Puget Sound. She took a breath and turned back to Gage and Aidan who were sitting at a small round table. She joined them, and Gage immediately placed his hand on her thigh, its warm heat comforting and stimulating at once. Now was definitely not the time to get worked up over Gage, but his kiss had stirred up the ever-present charge between them. Not to mention that all he had to do was exist in space near her, and that hot, electric charge slid through her veins. She took a breath and focused on the moment.

Aidan turned to her, his blue eyes sharp and assessing. "How are you feeling about this?"

"Okay, I guess. I mean, not great, but it'd be weird if I felt good about it. It's not talking to the police, it's just the whole thing. Has anyone actually talked to Kent?"

Aidan shook his head. "The plan is for the police to interview you and see if anything comes up that might give them some clues about the robbery. Then they plan to bring Kent in for questioning. I can sit with you during the interview with them…"

Gage cut Aidan off. "I'll be there too." His eyes were dark when he spoke.

Aidan looked at Gage and back at Marley. "Gage, I know you want to be there, but I'm not sure that's a good idea."

"Why?" Gage all but barked his question.

Marley's stomach churned. She'd somehow managed to tamp down her anxiety about why she was here most of last night and this morning. She'd shrouded herself in a cloud of denial. Discussing what was coming brought her feelings to the fore. She couldn't quite believe Kent would have gone so far as to assault and rob her, but the fact was someone had. Her heart raced and her skin got clammy. She remembered what her therapist had told her—to let the feelings happen and find something to anchor her to the present moment. Her therapist had told her that her body would eventually convince her mind that the fear wasn't coming to fruition in the present moment, but that it would take practice and patience. She focused on the feel of Gage's hand on her leg and let the feelings pass through her. Right now, she was safe here beside Gage. She glanced at Gage who was glaring at Aidan.

"Look man, I get why you want to be in the interview with Marley, but she needs to not be worried about how you're feeling. And I know you'll be feeling something. You have every right to be furious at the guy who robbed and assaulted her, but the police need to be able to interview her without you unintentionally affecting her." Aidan paused and glanced at Marley. "Any thoughts on this?"

Marley appreciated that he was including her. She looked to Gage and reached for his hand. He took a slow breath, but remained silent. "Much as I want you right there with me, it's probably better if you're not. I already went through these interviews a few times, unless they plan to do something differently, they'll basically walk me through what I remember. I don't want to hold back anything unconsciously. You have no idea how much it means to me that you're helping with this. But if you start to get upset at what you hear, I'll be worried about you."

Gage held her gaze and swore softly. He turned to Aidan. "You promise I can wait right outside the room and you'll get me right away if she needs me?"

Aidan nodded firmly. "Absolutely."

Gage squeezed her hand and nodded firmly. "I don't like it, but I get it. What's the timeframe on when they'll interview Kent? I want to be there for that."

Aidan shrugged. "That depends. They don't want to tip him off, so it'll depend on if they can reach him right away for questioning. The lead detective's been great. He'll keep us in the loop every step of the way. They've got an angle beyond this they're working with him. The woman he had an affair with has reported he's been stalking her and making threats ever since she broke it off with him. Sounds like Kent's pretty pissed off that he's not getting a kickback for passing on data to her anymore."

Fear threaded through Marley. As disgusted as she was to learn what Kent had done, the more she learned about him, the more he frightened her. She only hoped the police would be able to arrest him soon. The conversation moved on to lighter matters with Aidan discussing when he might be able to come to Last Frontier Lodge for a visit.

* * *

Gage waited outside the room where the police were interviewing Marley. While his mind was fully aware of why it wouldn't be helpful for him to be present during the interview, his emotions emphatically disagreed. After years of missions as a Navy SEAL, he knew damn well it was never a good idea for emotions to be in charge, but when it came to Marley, his definitely were. The only thing keeping him out of that room was the knowledge that Aidan was there with her. He trusted Aidan completely and knew Aidan would come get him if needed. Right before Marley had walked in the room, she'd squeezed his hand and met his eyes. Her clear, forest green gaze nearly undid him right then and there. She was trying so hard to be strong.

He checked his watch. It had only been fifteen minutes. He shackled his emotions and leaned his head against the wall. He was good at waiting and would wait as long as he had to. His phone vibrated in his pocket. He pulled it out to see Becca's number flash on the screen.

"Hey Becca. What's up?"

"Just calling to check in. We're wondering how Marley's doing."

Gage smiled to himself. After he'd filled Jessa and Becca in, they'd emphatically supported his decision to go with her to Seattle. Becca had gone into her protective bear mode, as she was prone to doing. As a prosecutor, she specialized in cases involving victims of violent crimes. Her skepticism about Marley, already waning, had dissolved in the face of a cause. Marley had become her personal cause for the moment. She'd contacted the police this morning to get an update herself and demand that they make sure Marley was provided with all the support she needed.

"Marley's doing just fine. Thanks for asking. Honestly, I'm in worse shape than she is. They didn't think it was a great idea for me to be in the interview room with her since I might have some feelings about the situation, so I'm stuck waiting."

Becca chuckled. "Wow, you really love her, don't you?"

Gage thought perhaps he should argue the point with Becca, but it seemed silly. He wasn't the most comfortable with expressing his feelings, but it didn't dilute their depth. He sighed. "Yeah, pretty much. Not so sure what to do about it."

He could feel Becca's smile through the phone when she spoke. "Seems like you're doing what you need to do. If you ask me, she loves you too."

He couldn't help the uncertainty that flared in his heart. He was truly walking on foreign ground with Marley. He'd never once in his life experienced uncertainty when it came to a woman. He'd always been confident that he didn't want serious emotional entanglements, so he didn't have them. It had been simple and clean that way. Then he met Marley. All the rules he'd lived by went out the window with her. He was so rattled by how much she meant to him, he didn't know how to talk to her about it. To say he was out of practice was an understatement. He hadn't had any practice at this kind of thing. He took a slow breath.

"You think so, huh?"

"As much as I can guess based on how she looks when she talks about you and when you get anywhere near her. She lights up like a top. I've only known her a few days, and I'm the first person to be skeptical, but you two are so obvious, it almost hurts to watch."

"I know I don't talk much about stuff like this…"

Becca interjected. "I'd say it's more that you never talked much about stuff like this because you've never had stuff like this in your life," she countered with a soft chuckle.

"Any advice?"

"Tell her how you feel. Maybe not today

because you two have a lot of other things to focus on, but soon."

"That simple, huh?"

"In some ways, it is," she said softly.

"Okay." They sat quietly on the phone for a long moment.

Becca spoke again. "Will you call us when you have an update?"

Gage was touched at Becca's concern for Marley, but he shouldn't have been surprised. Becca thrived when she had someone to focus on, someone to worry about. He chuckled this time. "Of course. You know we're flying back tomorrow morning, right?"

"Of course. We're picking you up at the airport. But a lot can happen between now and then."

"So true, so true." Gage said goodbye and hung up. He flipped the phone idly in his hand, considering his conversation with Becca. He knew she was right, but he wasn't so sure she could quite comprehend how out of his depth he was with Marley. He thought back on the many times he'd teased his team members for losing their heads over a woman and felt like he should call in a few apologies. He'd been utterly oblivious to the cataclysmic effects of falling in love. Marley had been nowhere near the map he'd created for his life when he planned his move to Diamond Creek to reopen Last Frontier Lodge. Now, he couldn't imagine life without her.

With a sigh, he leaned his head against the wall again, wondering when Marley would be out. As if he'd conjured her, the door to the interview room opened and she walked out, Aidan close behind her. Gage stood and turned to her. Her eyes were shuttered and tired. She looked on edge. He started toward her, but she waved him away.

"Where's the restroom?" she asked abruptly.

Aidan pointed down the hall, and she walked briskly to the restroom and pushed through the door. Gage turned to Aidan. "Is she okay?"

Aidan shrugged. "You know her much better than I do. She handled the interview okay, but it's not an easy subject. I'm not sure how much she's told you."

"She glossed over the details. I heard more from a family friend and another friend of hers. Not that it wouldn't bother me, but if it was just a robbery, it'd be a lot easier to stomach. The guy pistol whipped her and threw her in a corner though—every time I think about that part, I almost blow my lid." Gage marshaled his composure, calling on his reserves to keep it together. He met Aidan's eyes. "Anything new come out of it?"

"Maybe a few details. I'm gonna pop back in and see what they have to say now, but I wanted to walk her out here. If you wait here, I'll update you."

Gage nodded and watched Aidan walk back into the interview room where the detectives were waiting. He glanced down the hall, impatient for Marley to return. A few minutes ticked by and then she came through the door and walked toward him. She stopped in front of him, and he felt the tension radiating from her. His throat tight, he stepped to her and pulled her into his arms.

"I'm fine," she said, her voice muffled against his shoulder.

She leaned her head back to look up at him. Her eyes were still tired, but her gaze was softer, less edgy than it had been when she first came out.

"Let's sit down," she said tugging him by the hand.

He joined her, his arm firmly around her shoulders. "Do you want to talk about it?" he asked.

She shook her head. "Not much to say really. I'm glad you're here." She took a quick breath. "Aidan said he'd check with them and let me know what's next."

"He will," Gage said firmly.

They waited quietly while Gage grappled with a new reality for him. There was a time when he couldn't have fathomed that his emotions would run the show, but the opposite was true now. With Marley, how he felt drove everything he did.

It wasn't too long before Aidan stepped out with the lead detective, Officer Phillips. Officer Phillips reported only that he'd head out with a partner later this afternoon to bring Kent in for questioning. After they departed, Aidan offered additional details, namely that Marley had been able to confirm a scar she'd seen on her assailant's hand. What she hadn't known was that it matched a scar on Kent's hand.

Up to that point, Gage had somehow managed to keep his fury toward Kent in check. But when suspicion ballooned into reality, the fury thundered back. He stood up and started down the hall, Aidan on his heels and Marley running after both of them.

CHAPTER 20

Marley ran into the parking garage, racing to catch up to Gage and Aidan. As she came around the corner to the row of cars where they'd parked their rental car, she saw Gage paused by the car. The driver's side door was open and he was poised to climb in. Aidan was saying something, but Gage looked past him, his eyes locking onto her. He waited until she reached his side.

Out of breath, she came to a halt and gulped in air. "Gage, where are you going?"

He reached over, his hand threading into her hair. He tugged her close for a quick, searing kiss and then pulled back, his hand sliding out of her hair and cupping her cheek. "Stay with Aidan. I'm going to take care of something."

Marley stared at him. "Don't go after Kent," she said, afraid that was his intent.

Gage held her gaze, his gray eyes flashing like lightning. "You don't need to worry about me doing anything stupid, but I'll make sure Kent never hurts you again."

Before she could open her mouth to reply, he swung away and slammed the car door shut, shifting into reverse and peeling out of the parking garage. Marley turned to Aidan.

"Let's go," she said. All she could think was they had to follow Gage and stop him. What she knew about Kent at this point scared her, and she didn't want Gage putting himself in the middle.

Aidan glanced down at her, his blue eyes assessing. "No," he said flatly.

Marley tried to argue the point, but Aidan was implacable. He escorted her back to their hotel room and sat quietly at the table while she paced back and forth. His phone rang. After he glanced at the screen, he looked to her.

"I need to take this. I'll be in the hall. You okay for a few minutes?"

Marley nodded. She felt tossed and turned inside with the tumult of emotions inside. She was dealing with the aftermath of once again recounting the events the night of the robbery, along with coming to terms that it was becoming frighteningly real that a man she'd known had robbed and assaulted her. On top of that, she was worried about Gage. He'd felt coiled so tight at the police station, she thought he might explode. Energy came off of him in waves.

There was a sharp knock at the door. Marley swung the door open, assuming it was Aidan. Her heart froze when she saw Kent in the doorway. He looked ragged. His dark blonde hair was mussed, his tie loosened and his jacket hanging open. She gasped. Without a word, Kent pushed into her, kicking the door shut behind him. She tried to scream, but her voice was trapped. Kent shoved her against the wall, his elbow pressing against her throat.

"You stupid fucking bitch! Who the hell did you send to my house?"

Fear crashed through her. She felt frozen

inside—all she could manage was to shake her head. Kent shoved her again, the pressure against her throat crushing. She struggled to breathe. Her vision blurred and she lost focus. Kent kept ranting and swearing, but she couldn't hear. All she could think was she wished she'd told Gage she loved him.

There was a bang against the door. Suddenly the pressure on her throat disappeared when the door crashed open, the frame splintering as it did. Gage plowed into Kent. She collapsed against the wall, gulping air in. In a blur, Gage grabbed Kent by the collar, yanking him off his feet and throwing him up against the wall. Aidan was right behind Gage. He kicked the broken door shut and stood in front of it.

Gage held Kent against the wall almost effortlessly. His gray eyes were flat as he stared at Kent. Kent struggled against Gage's grip. "Who the hell are you?"

"Doesn't matter who I am." Gage's voice was low and laced with fury.

Kent glanced at Aidan and over to Marley, his eyes wild.

Aidan said nothing. Marley stared at Kent, the fear still pounding through her, but slowly abating now that Gage and Aidan were here. "Why are you here?" she finally asked, wondering how Kent had known she was here in this particular hotel room.

"I need that fucking flash drive!"

Gage tightened his grip on Kent's shirt, shoving him harder against the wall. He glanced at Marley and nodded, making her realize he was giving her the chance to ask questions if she chose.

She looked at Kent, her stomach queasy. "How come you've been pretending like those emails were from HR if they were from you?"

"Because I need the damn flash drive, that's why."

Marley realized Kent was still oblivious to the ongoing police investigation and un-aware he was already facing legal trouble.

"Why do you think I have the flash drive?"

"Because I hid it in your damn apart-ment, that's why. The last time you were out of town and Becky watered your plants, I went with her. I needed to make sure it was somewhere safe. Your apartment was per-fect because no one would connect it to me. What the hell did you do with it?"

Marley shook her head slowly, glancing between Aidan and Gage before looking back at Kent. Gage still held him easily, almost casually. At a glance, Aidan appeared to be lounging against the hotel room door, but she knew he was ready to back Gage up in a split second if needed.

"I didn't do anything with it. I never knew it was there. Where did you hide it?"

"Inside your dictionary. You had it way up on the top shelf, so I figured you didn't use it much." Kent kicked against Gage. "Who the hell are you? You showed up at my house. That's how I found Marley. By following you back here, dumbass."

Gage's nostrils flared, but he barely moved as he pressed his forearm against Kent's throat. He remained silent and nodded to Marley to continue.

"Well, no wonder you couldn't find it when you robbed my place. I took a load of books to the big library sale a few weeks before. Your flash drive went with them." Marley paused as she considered her next question. She glanced to Aidan. "How much does he know?" she asked, angling her head toward Kent.

"Doesn't matter. Say whatever you want."

"Why did you have to hurt me?" Marley asked, fighting the rush of anxiety that welled inside. She reminded herself she was safe now. Gage and Aidan wouldn't let anything happen.

Kent slammed his head against the wall, struggling against Gage. Gage swiftly slammed back. Marley wondered if Gage would tire, but he seemed too amped up for that to happen.

"You weren't supposed to be there," Kent choked out. "If you hadn't shown up, it would have been no big deal. I just needed that flash drive back."

Marley felt sick as she stared at Kent. "But why?"

"Because it had info I needed to keep. That's all," Kent said flatly.

He suddenly arched his back and kicked out, managing to break free from Gage's grip. As Kent stumbled to the floor and attempted to bolt past Gage, Gage leaned back and drove his fist into Kent's face. Aidan's only move was to straighten his stance. He completely blocked the door, so there was no way for Kent to easily leave. Kent fell against the wall and tried to swing at Gage, but missed completely. Gage grabbed him by the collar again and held him high. "Here's the deal: you just gave us exactly what we need to make sure you're locked up. And this is for Marley." He drove his fist into Kent's face again, literally pulling Kent forward into his fist as he did. Blood spurted from Kent's nose. Gage pulled his arm back again when there was a pounding on the door, the police announcing their presence.

Gage dropped his arm, but didn't release Kent. The police barged into the room, immediately taking over and cuffing Kent. Marley was separated from Gage and Aidan as they were respectively questioned. Much later, after they'd returned to the police station for more follow up, Marley walked back into the hotel room with Gage. He'd called ahead and asked the hotel to clean their room. The door had already been repaired and the room was tidy. Marley tossed her jacket and purse in a chair and sat on the edge of the bed with a sigh.

Gage had been quiet to the point of brooding ever since the incident with Kent. He threw his jacket on top of hers and walked to the window, his hands tucked in his pockets. She considered what to say. In a few short hours, the weight of her robbery and assault had been lifted since she now knew for certain who had done it and why. She would still be stuck with the aftereffects, but at least she no longer had to wonder. Her body was tired and wired at once. Emotionally, she was overwhelmed. She didn't know how to thank Gage, as he'd been the one to ask for Aidan's help and had stepped in without hesitation today.

She was nervous and uncertain why he was so quiet and withdrawn. It was enough that she was stumbling about while her feelings for him grew by the day. His actions the past few days wound the invisible threads between them tighter. She couldn't quite fathom what to do with her feelings. She recalled Becca's comment that it was clear Gage loved her. Marley watched him, her heart in her throat.

"Gage."

He turned away from the window, his eyes immediately on her. His expression was guarded.

"Are you okay?" She forced herself to speak, even though she was nervous.

He nodded sharply. "Are you?"

She held his gaze, willing her nerves to settle, as she stood and approached him. "I'm fine. Thank you for everything today. If it wasn't for you and Aidan, I don't know if we'd ever have found out what happened."

She stepped in front of him and gasped when he tugged her close, engulfing her in a tight embrace. She tucked her head into his shoulder and just held on. She could feel his heartbeat, beating in time with hers. Tension hummed in his body, his muscles were taut, his breathing labored. She pulled back and glanced up. His smoky eyes met hers. He loosened his hold and stroked a hand up her back. "You don't need to thank me," he said, his voice gravelly.

"Are you sure you're okay?"

His shoulders rose and fell with a deep breath. "Yeah. Sorry if I seem tense. It took everything I had not to beat Kent senseless. The only thing holding me back was knowing it wouldn't do you any good for me to be sitting in jail alongside him. Not to mention, I knew Aidan wouldn't let me do anything stupid, and he's strong enough to stop me if he had to," he said wryly.

Marley's pulse ricocheted wildly when

Gage looked back down at her. He cleared his throat. "I'm used to being in control. When it comes to you, not so much. I love you, you know."

His words, gruff with a tinge of vulnerability, seared through her. Her heart swelled and tears filled her eyes. His somber, austere expression softened as he brought a hand around and stroked his thumb across the tear that rolled down her cheek. She tried to speak, but no words came out. Joy crashed through her in a wave. She reached up, cupping his face in her hands, and smiled through her tears. "I love you too...I've been wondering what to do about that." Shyness followed her words. Her hands slid down his cheeks, coming to rest on his chest. His heart thudded against her palm.

Gage's mouth quirked in a small smile. "Well, that's good to know. I, uh, don't have too much experience with this kind of thing. I figured since I almost lost my mind over you today, I might as well get over myself and tell you how I felt."

She bit her lip as she studied him. This man, so strong, so sexy and so handsome, had stolen her heart. Seeing him look vulnerable tugged at her deep inside. She curled her hand around the back of his neck and pulled him down to meet her for a kiss.

* * *

MARLEY CAUGHT her bottom lip with her teeth, and Gage thought he might explode. He wasn't sure how declarations of love were supposed to go, but all he wanted right now was to bury himself so deep inside of her, he forgot where she began and he ended. He'd spent the entire afternoon on edge, barely able to keep himself sane. When he saw Kent pinning Marley to the wall, rage had almost blinded him. It had taken every ounce of willpower he had to remember he needed to keep it together for Marley. He was relieved beyond measure Aidan had been present because he'd known he could count on Aidan to make sure things didn't go too far.

He was so proud of Marley. She'd kept it together through everything today. He looked down at her. Her forest green eyes were bright with tears. He hadn't counted on her telling him she loved him, but when she said the words, his heart felt like it was going to explode. When she tugged him down for a kiss, he let go.

He dove into the warm sweetness of her mouth, delving and stroking, savoring the wild tangle with her tongue. He laced a hand in her hair while the other stroked down her back and cupped her lush bottom, pulling her against his arousal. She gasped in his mouth, and he tore his lips free, pausing for a moment to look at her. Her eyes were pools of heat, her lips kiss-swollen, and her cheeks flushed. Lust surged inside, tightening its hold on him. He traced her mouth with his thumb. Her breath came out in gasp, and he was lost. He wanted to taste every inch of her. He molded his mouth over hers again for a deep, hot kiss before nipping her earlobe, savoring the shiver that followed. He tore at her blouse as his lips traveled down the side of her neck and traced the edge of her collarbone. When a button caught, he tore at the fabric, swearing until it gave, the button tearing out and bouncing against the wall.

Her lacy black bra awaited him. Glimpses of her pink nipples teased him through the lace. He closed his mouth over one, groaning against her when she arched into him and whispered his name. He teased her nipples until the lace was drenched and they were hard and pebbled. Shoving her blouse off of her shoulders, he finally flicked the clasp between her breasts. The coil of longing tightened inside when her full breasts tumbled free. He cupped them in his hands, rolling her nipples in his fingers. Her breath was ragged as she arched into his hands. He took a step back and she followed, shoving his shirt up. He reached behind his head, lifting it off in one move.

Marley stepped closer and ran her hands up his chest before dragging them back down to stroke his arousal. He was so hard, he could have come right then and there, but he latched onto his control, his breath hissing through his teeth when she unbuttoned his fly and curled a palm around his cock. He walked backwards until his knees bumped against the bed. Sitting, he pulled her between his legs and drew a nipple into his mouth again. He toyed with the other as he sucked and nipped, alternating between them until she was gasping and writhing against him. Lust drummed through him and longing lashed at him as he paused to look at her. Her auburn hair was rumpled, her lips kiss swollen, and her skin dewy. He traced the paths of freckles dotting her skin and almost lost it when her breath hitched.

Gage tore at her jeans and shoved them down around her ankles. Marley kicked them out of the way and stood bare before him save her black lace panties. He'd come to know that while she tended to dress practically, she had a penchant for black lace, which nearly drove him mad. He cupped her mound with his palm and then stroked his thumb across the lace, his cock tightening at the moisture. He moved swiftly, lifting her and turning so she lay before him. Her breasts rose and fell with her ragged breathing. Hooking a finger over the edge of her thong, he dragged it off. He tugged on her knees until her bottom rested against the edge of the bed.

She pushed herself up and began to shove his jeans down.

"Not yet," he said, his voice breaking.

Marley paused and looked up at him, the bare longing in her gaze nearly breaking his control. He knelt between her knees and placed a palm between her breasts. She started to protest and then he stroked a finger through her folds, drenched with her desire. She arched and cried out, falling back against the bed. He set out to memorize every inch of the center of her, tracing her folds with his finger and then stroking in and out of her channel, which throbbed around his touch. She writhed and flexed against his hand and cried out again when he brought his mouth to her. She brought him to the very edge of his control when she arched into his mouth. He forced himself to hold on because he meant for her to climb higher than she ever had. He kept up a relentless pace of strokes, his fingers and tongue delving into her channel, coasting over her clit until she pleaded with him. When he felt her begin to convulse around his fingers, he dragged his tongue across her clit and brought it into his mouth with just enough suction that she screamed and came apart against his mouth. He slowed his stroking until her hips relaxed.

Only then did he stand. She lay before him—rosy, scattered with freckles and flushed all over. She leaned up on her elbows and met his eyes, hers dark with passion. Holding her gaze, he shoved his jeans down, stepping out of them as he knelt on the bed.

* * *

MARLEY FELT the mattress give under Gage's weight when his knee came down on the bed. His smoky gaze held her. He'd just brought her to a mind-shattering climax, leaving her almost limp in the aftermath. But when she'd looked up to find him standing and shoving his jeans down, desire kept beating its drum. He stood bare before her, his body sheer perfection—hard, bronzed muscle. When he leaned forward, she moved swiftly, shimmying out from under him, shoving him down and straddling him. In the tangle, she rested atop, her wet center astride his hard shaft. His breath came in sharply when he met her eyes. Though she was desperate to feel him inside of her, she forced herself to hold still and began to roll her hips back and forth slowly. The feel of him against her almost brought her to another orgasm, but she held on.

Gage brought a hand up, curling it around her neck and slowly pulling her forward. His lips caught hers in a searing kiss, breaking away when he slid his hand between them and poised his cock to rest in her folds. He held her by the hip in his iron grip.

"Marley…"

She dragged her eyes open to meet his gaze.

"Now," he whispered fiercely.

He surged into her, driving deeply. She cried out, pleasure rippling through her as he filled her and stretched her. He loosened his grip and she began to move, sliding up and down the length of him. They fell into a rhythm, his hand curled on her hip as she rode him. She rolled up and down the length of him, savoring how he filled and stretched her. His breathing became more ragged, his hips rising to meet hers. Everything blurred, but the feel of him inside her. She raced toward the edge, pleasure spiking higher and higher with each driving thrust. She forced herself to hold on until she felt him arch more deeply into her, driving to the hilt. The delicious pressure broke free and she came apart, shuddering around him as he cried out. His arms came around her and he pulled her down against his chest. She was wrung through and fell against him.

She felt the beat of his heart against her.

She tucked her head in the crook of his shoulder. His palm stroked in slow circles on her back as their breathing slowed. After several long moments, she lifted her head. His eyes opened. With a hint of a grin, he smoothed her hair with his hand. "All I meant to do was tell you I love you."

Gage walked through the kitchen at the lodge and couldn't hold back his smile. It was Christmas Eve. Though the kitchen was empty at the moment with Delia and her crew done until the day after Christmas, the room was scented with holiday cooking and baking. Gage pushed through the door into the restaurant and ran smack into Garrett, Becca's twin brother and the last of his family members to arrive.

"Damn glad you made it," Gage said, giving Garrett a swift hug before stepping back.

Garrett met his eyes and smiled wryly. "My flight was late, but I'm here. Place looks great," Garrett commented as he looked around the restaurant. Garrett stood shoulder to shoulder with Gage. He shared his twin sister's glossy dark hair though he kept his cropped close to his head. His sharp blue eyes landed on Gage. "Sorry I missed you when you stopped by last week. Didn't know you were coming to Seattle."

Gage shrugged. "It wasn't exactly a visiting trip. I stopped by your place on my way back to the airport, figuring I'd chance it." Gage hadn't expected Garrett to be home, seeing as Garrett took the idea of being a workaholic way too seriously. He was a high-flying lawyer, specializing in corporate law, and worked at a relentless pace. Gage was pleased Garrett managed to stop working long enough to come up to Last Frontier Lodge for the holidays. If Gage's guess was right, Garrett heard an earful from Becca and their mother about it.

"Did you already find your room?" Gage asked.

"Yup. Becca showed me."

Gage looked past Garrett to the far side of the restaurant by the windows. Becca and Jessa had arranged several tables together for a family dinner. Becca was deep in conversation with their mother, Jill. Jessa was filling wineglasses. Sawyer, his youngest brother, was in the midst of a game of cards with their father, Gage Sr. Gage had invited Marley and her parents, along with Don's family, over for a shared dinner. He was keyed up about her meeting his whole family. Collectively, they were a handful, tending toward boisterous. He was relieved she'd had some time to get to know Becca and Jessa first.

He hooked his arm over Garrett's shoulder. "Come on, let's eat."

As they made their way across the room, Gage glanced out the windows and saw Marley walking up the stairs to the back deck. Garrett followed his gaze and glanced at Gage, his blue eyes tinged with amusement. "That must be Marley. According to Becca, you're in love. Gotta say, I thought she must be joking, but with the way you look at her, I'm reconsidering."

Gage shrugged. "Becca's right."

Garrett's brows hitched and his eyes widened. "Wow. And here I considered you my role model, above all that messy relationship business."

Gage chuckled. "I've discovered all it

takes is the right woman." He broke away from Garrett and strode to the door by the deck. Delia had kept the housekeeping staff busy decorating this week and bells jingled when he opened the door. Sleigh bells and spruce wreaths were affixed to every door. Gage and Don had chipped in and spent an entire afternoon on ladders hanging holiday lights on the lodge. A gorgeous spruce tree had been decorated at the front outside. It had taken Becca and Jessa an entire afternoon to decorate it while they wrangled assistance from Gage and Don for the upper portions of the tree. The inside of the lodge was filled with clusters of greenery, red ribbons, and mistletoe hanging in archways.

He waited as Marley walked across the deck in the wispy light of dusk. The sun had fallen behind the mountains already, faint streaks of red and gold arcing across the sky. Marley's boots crunched in the thin layer of snow on the deck. A gust of wind caught her hair and swirled it behind her. When she reached the door, she was smiling. Gage tugged her into his arms and kissed her, her lips warming under his. He forgot they had an audience and lost himself in the feel of her in his arms.

The sound of a throat clearing broke him out of his haze and he pulled away. Marley was flushed when he gripped her hand and tugged her inside. When he turned, he found Sawyer standing nearby. Sawyer grinned when he met Gage's eyes. "Figured somebody had to get your attention."

Looking at Sawyer was like looking at a younger version of himself. Sawyer shared his brown hair and gray eyes. Since he'd followed Gage into the Navy and also become a Navy SEAL, he was in impeccable physical condition.

Sawyer turned his attention to Marley. "You must be Marley. Very nice to meet you," Sawyer said, leaning over to kiss Marley on the cheek, a teasing glint in his eyes.

Marley flushed. "Nice to meet you too."

"Watch out for him," Gage commented. "Sawyer is a relentless flirt."

Sawyer's grin deepened. He shrugged unabashedly. "No need to worry. Anyone that can steal Gage's heart isn't possibly going to let me steal her away."

Marley glanced between them. Gage

tugged her to his side. "Come on, let me introduce you to the rest of my family."

* * *

MARLEY LOOKED around the room and sighed. Gage's entire family was there, along with her parents, Lacey, and the Peters family. Gage's mother, Jill, had orchestrated a full dinner. Marley had enough wine that she floated in a soft warmth. Gage had hardly left her side tonight and sat with her now, his arm draped across the back of her chair, his fingers absently toying with her hair. He was in the midst of mediating a friendly debate between Garrett and Becca over the merits of lawyers. Marley found it fascinating that they were twins who'd both become lawyers and yet had taken almost opposing career paths with Garrett catering to the wealthy corporate world, while Becca was passionate about working with underprivileged clients.

She glanced around the table and saw Delia flush. When she followed Delia's gaze, Marley found it led straight to Garrett who appeared momentarily distracted. He said something to Gage and then his eyes bounced to Delia, his blue gaze curious.

After dinner was finished and most of the guests had left, Marley wiped her hands on a towel and made her way out of the kitchen. Gage stood beside his mother, leaning against the wall by the archway leading from the restaurant out to the reception area. His mother reached up and gave him a kiss on the cheek, handing him something that Gage immediately slipped in his pocket. Jill stepped away and walked past him into the other room.

Marley made her way to Gage's side, curiosity pecking at her thoughts. He lifted his head when he heard her approach, his gray gaze darkening. He didn't move, but held a hand out and tugged her to him, immediately fitting his mouth over hers in a scorching kiss. Her pulse skittered, heat unfurling inside. The air shimmered between them, alive with the electric current that buzzed to life whenever she was near him.

When he pulled away, his eyes stayed on her, intent and somber at once. He appeared to be considering something. "What is it?" she asked.

He cleared his throat. "I've been thinking..." He paused and shook his head sharply. "In case you haven't noticed, I'm not too poetic. Here goes..." He slid his hand into his pocket. He held still for a moment, his eyes bearing into hers. Marley could barely breathe as the heat of his gaze seared into her. Flutters built in her core, her heart pounding in anticipation.

He opened his hand. She gasped. A beautiful ring sat glittering on his palm. "I meant to get a box for it, but I didn't have time today. I asked my mom to bring it up with her. It's my grandmother's wedding ring." He took a breath, his eyes usually so confident, holding a glimmer of vulnerability. "I love you. I can't imagine life without you, so I figure I might as well try to make it official as soon as I can. Will you marry me?"

Marley gasped at the wave of joy that crested inside. Tears pricked her eyes. Gage waited, his gaze never breaking from hers. She finally managed to gather herself enough to answer. "Yes, yes!" She threw her arms around him. Gage reflexively caught her in his strong embrace, lifting her against him.

"For a second there, I wasn't sure," he said, his voice muffled against her hair.

She leaned back and cupped his cheeks in her hands, dusting kisses on his face. "There was never any doubt."

She wiggled in his arms, and he loosened his hold, allowing her to slide down his body. She held her hand out, and Gage slipped the ring over the finger. The diamond glittered from the reflection of the holiday lights hanging in the archway.

GAGE AWOKE on Christmas morning with Marley curled tight against him. He rolled his head to the side and looked out the cabin windows. A fresh coating of snow had fallen during the night. The landscape sparkled under the sun. After coffee, they walked through the trees to the lodge. The spruce forest was dusted with snow, the air sharp and crisp. When they walked into the lodge, the air was scented with cider and holiday baking. Jessa squealed when she saw them, racing across the room to engulf Marley in a hug.

"All I need to know is when!" Jessa exclaimed when she finally let Marley go.

Marley met his eyes and shrugged, her

cheeks bright. "Um, we haven't gotten that far."

Gage looped his arm across Marley's shoulder and grinned at Jessa. "I know you're ready to plan our wedding down to the last detail, but let's enjoy today first. Merry Christmas," he said, leaning over to drop a kiss on Jessa's cheek.

Jessa huffed, but her smile held. "Fine. I'll wait, but don't make me wait too long."

Jessa hurried off while Gage and Marley followed at a slower pace. They were instantly engulfed in the rush of the morning. Marley's parents had happily accepted the offer to spend Christmas Day at the lodge. Lacey had badgered Don into getting one of the lifts going for the day so friends and family could ski. After a boisterous breakfast and presents had been handed around, Gage stood by while Marley's mother hugged her tightly after spying the ring on her finger. Marley's father, Stan, clapped him on the back.

"Knew the first time I saw you with her that Marley found a good man," Stan offered gruffly. "She's had a tough year." Stan cleared his throat and met Gage's eyes. After a long moment, he tugged him in for a quick hug before stepping away to drop a kiss on Marley's cheek. Stan had stopped by the lodge last week after they got back from Seattle and thanked Gage for his help in bringing Kent to justice for what he did to Marley. Gage recognized Stan for a man of few words, but it was clear he loved his daughter deeply and had been distraught to see her go through what she did.

Gage watched Marley, her auburn curls bright in the sun that fell across her. After her mother moved on, he stepped to her side, resisting the urge to pull her close for a kiss. He was buzzing with emotion girded by desire. Ever since he'd finally let himself feel what he felt for Marley and she'd actually agreed to marry him, he was struggling to contain himself. He'd become accustomed to the almost constant state of arousal he experienced whenever Marley was near, but it was rather inconvenient when they were surrounded by family and friends.

Marley glanced up and smiled. "Let's ski." She grabbed his hand and tugged him to the hallway where they quickly tossed outerwear on. The deck was scattered with skis and boots. Gage made a beeline for the small shed on the corner of the deck where he'd stored a set of skis for himself and Marley. As they rode up the lift together, his heart swelled. He'd somehow managed to pull off his childhood dream of living at the lodge again and stumbled into the woman of his dreams at the same time.

The air was crisp and cold. As the lift crested the top of the slope, Kachemak Bay glittered ahead, the sun striking sparks on its surface. The mountains across stood tall and quiet, snowy against the bright blue sky. An eagle screeched nearby. Gage looked around and saw the eagle take flight off of its perch atop the ski hut. Its wings cast a shadow across the snow as it angled into the breeze before flying out of sight. The lift came to a smooth stop. He and Marley had been alone on this ride up, but the slope held at least half of their respective families. Laughter drifted on the cold breeze.

Marley paused once they were off the lift and glanced back at him briefly. She lifted a ski pole in a wave and then turned away, expertly zigzagging her way down the slope. Gage watched her for a moment, her auburn hair blowing behind her. He pushed off and followed her down. He savored the speed and leaned into the turns as he made his way down. Marley was fast and held her speed ahead of him. She came to a swirling stop at the bottom, snow flying up around her. She waited, watching as he approached. He skied to her side. Without a beat, he brought his lips to hers and delved into the warm sweetness of her mouth. A soft thud hit his back and he pulled away, turning to see Sawyer grinning from a distance before he turned away and lobbed a snowball toward Garrett.

Gage chuckled and turned back to Marley. Her forest green eyes were bright and her cheeks flushed. She bit her lip, her eyes considering. "What if we got married today?"

His heart thumped—hard. "Today?"

She nodded, a slow smile spreading across her face. "Why not? In Alaska, anyone can marry a couple in Alaska once. We can do the ceremony today and file the paperwork when the clerk's office is open after the holiday."

Gage's chest suddenly felt tight. He wanted nothing more than this today, but he didn't want Marley to feel rushed. "Are you sure? And how is it anyone can marry people in Alaska?" He couldn't help but ask because it seemed almost too easy.

Marley grinned. "It's that way because so much of Alaska is so rural, it's sometimes the only way for people to get married. I could care less about a big ceremony. It makes me anxious just thinking about it. Let's have Jessa help with the ceremony and ask Becca to do the actual marrying part. She's the one who told me you loved me and helped me get over myself."

Gage closed his eyes and took a breath, the bracing air grounding him. When he opened his eyes, all he saw was Marley's face. He nodded and leaned in for a swift kiss. "So, you wanna tell Jessa, or should I?"

Marley giggled. "I'll find Jessa. You go ask Becca about her part."

CHAPTER 22

It was early evening by the time the impromptu wedding had been orchestrated. Along with their collective families, the Peters family joined in with Delia offering to help cook a wedding meal, and Ginger joining the group to serve alongside Lacey as a bridesmaid.

Hours later after the vows had been exchanged and the lodge restaurant had emptied, Marley stood by the windows and looked out into the darkness. The moon rose above the mountains, its silvery light limning the landscape in a soft glow. The stars were so bright, she felt as if she could reach out and touch them. She heard her name and turned to see Gage leaning in the archway across the restaurant. He tilted his head, gesturing for her. She made her way across the room, feeling as if she was living in a fairytale. The only light came from the moon and the holiday lights. The archway where Gage stood was backlit by holiday lights from the reception area behind him.

When she got near, he pushed away from the wall and pulled her into his strong embrace. He buried his face in her hair, his hand stroking through it. "Thank you," he said, his voice muffled.

"For what?"

He pulled back, his smoky gaze locking on her. "Just everything. I didn't plan on falling in love, but here you are. I feel like the luckiest man in the world that you happen to love me too." He took a breath and glanced up. "I had to kiss you under the mistletoe. Someone told me it meant we'd live a long and peaceful life."

He traced her lips with his fingertip and cupped her cheek, bringing his mouth against hers in slow motion. His kiss started as gentle, but quickly became hot and deep. By the time he pulled away, liquid need was pulsing through her body and her heart was so full, she thought she might burst.

Without a word, he slid his hand down her arm, curling his hand around hers. They walked outside for the short walk to her cabin, as his family had occupied the entire private apartment and the few rooms set aside for them. Tomorrow the first guests to the lodge in many years would arrive.

For now, Marley and Gage walked hand and hand through the forest, the moonlight filtering through the trees, lighting their way. A bit later, Marley curled up beside Gage, resting her head on his shoulder. A soft happiness unfurled in her heart. Gage stroked a hand in her hair, his lips landing on her forehead. "Love you..." he mumbled, his breath instantly shifting into sleep.

EPILOGUE

*E*xactly one year later, Marley stood inside the living room at the lodge, looking outside. The slope was dotted with the bright colors of ski gear, filled with her and Gage's families and locals. Christmas afternoon was for locals only. They'd considered keeping it closed for the day, but the collective chorus from Diamond Creek residents was such that they had volunteers manning the lifts and slopes for the day. Marley picked Gage out of the crowd when he came flying down the slope and swirled to a stop. Lacey was hot on his heels and shook her fist at him as she passed by. They'd developed a friendly rivalry recently and were frequently challenging each other to races. As far as Marley could tell, they were even though she eschewed any discussion of it because she'd quickly discovered if she mentioned it, both would argue with her about why each was respectively faster than the other.

Meanwhile, Marley was sidelined from skiing for now. She ran her hand over her belly and felt another kick. She was eight months pregnant and more than ready to have their baby. Seeing Gage making his way to the lodge, she walked downstairs to meet him. Gage strode inside, and her breath caught in her throat. All he had to do was show up and her pulse went wild. He oozed masculinity. He walked across the room, his sculpted chest and abdomen outlined by his fitted skiing shirt. His gray eyes landed on hers, striking the flint of her desire. Even eight months pregnant, he managed to steal her senses.

He walked up to her, his mouth quirking in a half-smile as he stroked his hand over her very round belly. "How are we doing?" he asked, dropping his mouth for a quick kiss, sweeping his tongue inside her mouth and pulling away, catching her bottom lip between his teeth. His eyes held a wicked glint.

"We're fine. Have you noticed that I'm gigantic and I walk like a duck now?"

Gage shrugged. "You look beautiful."

Marley giggled. "For someone who said they didn't have any experience at relationships, you're a master."

Hours later, after another Christmas dinner with family and friends, Marley looked across the restaurant to find Gage standing beneath the archway again. Once again, time felt suspended. Moonlight filtered into the room. Holiday lights glittered outside. She walked slowly across the room, his smoky gaze a magnet for her. When she reached his side, she glanced up at the mistletoe hanging above. "I suppose we can't have an anniversary without a kiss under the mistletoe."

Gage ducked his head and brought his lips to hers, his touch gentle and scorching at once. When he pulled away, he rested his forehead against hers. "Merry Christmas."

Thank you for reading Take Me Home - I hope you loved Marley & Gage's story!

Up next in the Lodge Series is Garrett & Delia's story in Love at Last. Garrett Hamilton is a wealthy, corporate lawyer who has no time for romance. Swoon-worthy, sexy, and always in control, don't miss Garrett's story!

"Oh my! I am loving this series. They are hot and sexy, but sweet and romantic all rolled into one."

For more swoony & sassy romance, check out my website for the following stories: https://jhcroixauthor.com/books/

This Crazy Love kicks off the Swoon Series - small town southern romance with enough heat to melt you! Jackson & Shay's story is epic - swoon-worthy & intensely emotional. Jackson just happens to be Shay's brother's best friend. He's also *seriously* easy on the eyes. Shay has a past, the kind of past she would most definitely like to forget. Past or not, Jackson is about to rock her world. Don't miss their story! Free on all retailers!

Burn For Me is a second chance romance for the ages. Sexy firefighters? Check. Rugged men? Check. Wrapped up together? Check. Brave the fire in this hot, small-town romance. Amelia & Cade were high school sweethearts & then it all fell apart. When they cross paths again, it's epic - don't miss Cade's story!
Free on all retailers!

For more small town romance, take a visit to Last Frontier Lodge in Diamond Creek. A sexy, alpha SEAL meets his match with a brainy heroine in Take Me Home. Marley is all brains & Gage is all brawn. Sparks fly when their worlds collide. Don't miss Gage & Marley's story!
Free on all retailers!

If sports romance lights your spark, check out The Play. Liam is a British footballer who falls for Olivia, his doctor. A twist of forbidden heats up this swoon-worthy & laugh-out-loud romance. Don't miss Liam & Olivia's story.
Free on all retailers!

Sign up for my newsletter, so you can

receive information about upcoming new releases & receive a FREE copy of one of my books: http://jhcroixauthor.com/subscribe/

Thank you for reading Take Me Home! I hope you enjoyed the story. If so, you can help other readers find my books in a variety of ways.

1) Write a review!
2) Sign up for my newsletter, so you can receive information about upcoming new releases & receive a FREE copy of one of my books: http://jhcroixauthor.com/subscribe/
3) Like and follow my Amazon Author page at https://amazon.com/author/jhcroix
4) Follow me on Bookbub at https://www. bookbub.com/authors/j-h-croix
5) Follow me on Instagram at https://www. instagram.com/jhcroix/

6) Like my Facebook page at https://www.
facebook.com/jhcroix

* * *

Last Frontier Lodge Novels
Take Me Home
Love at Last
Just This Once
Falling Fast
Stay With Me
When We Fall
Hold Me Close
Crazy For You
Just Us
Dare With Me Series
Crash Into You
Evers & Afters
Come To Me - April 2021!
Back To Us - June 2021!
Swoon Series
This Crazy Love
Wait For Me
Break My Fall
Truly Madly Mine
Still Go Crazy
If We Dare
Steal My Heart

Into The Fire Series
Burn For Me
Slow Burn
Burn So Bad
Hot Mess
Burn So Good
Sweet Fire
Play With Fire
Melt With You
Burn For You
Crash & Burn
That Snowy Night
Brit Boys Sports Romance
The Play
Big Win
Out Of Bounds
Play Me
Naughty Wish
Diamond Creek Alaska Novels
When Love Comes
Follow Love
Love Unbroken
Love Untamed
Tumble Into Love
Christmas Nights

ACKNOWLEDGMENTS

*E*very book I write happens with great support from my husband who manages to make me laugh every day. Gracious thanks to Laura Kingsley, editor extraordinaire. Najla Qamber is responsible for this gorgeous cover. The biggest shout out goes to my readers – thank you, thank you!

xoxo

J.H. Croix

ABOUT THE AUTHOR

USA Today Bestselling Author J. H. Croix lives in a small town in the historical farmlands of Maine with her husband and two spoiled dogs. Croix writes contemporary romance with sassy women and rugged alpha men who aren't afraid to show some emotion. Her love for quirky small-towns and the characters that inhabit them shines through in her writing. Take a walk on the wild side of romance with her bestselling novels!

Places you can find me:
jhcroixauthor.com
jhcroix@jhcroix.com